Tale of Manaeth

Phillip D. Campbell III

Tale of Manaeth

By Phillip D. Campbell III

Published by
Cruachan Hill Press
1452 Lakeside Dr.
Howell, MI. 48843
http://www.taleofmanaeth.com
http://cruachanhill.blogspot.com

This book is a work of fiction. Names, characters, places and incidents are the product of this author's imagination. Any resemblance to actual persons, living or dead, is entirely coincidental.

Cover artwork by W.G. Price
Illustrations by Josie Lapczynski

Dedicated in honor of St. Joan of Arc, who after the Blessed Virgin is the purest and loveliest of all the holy virgins.

Guide to Pronounciation

Caeylon- Said with a soft "C" as in *celebrate*.

Manaeth- The dipthong "ae" is said with a long "a" and short "e" each enunciated – "ay-eh" (*Man' ay' eth*). Also the case in Saraeth.

Cyrian / Cyrenaica- Both said with a hard "C" as it *cat*.

Ú- Similar to English "oo" as in *food*.

Ö- Similar to English "ah" if standing alone, similar to "oo" (as in in *food* or *loon*) if preceded by another "o."

Tale of Manaeth

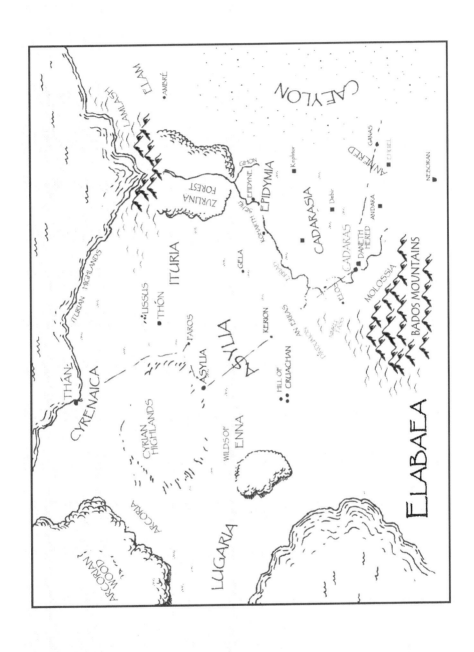

Chapter 1
Of Anathar and the Coming of the Marudans into Elabaea

It is told in the annals of the ancient days how it was their splendid horses that first brought the Elabaeans into the knowledge of the men of Maruda. For in those days, Anathar, king and lord of all Maruda, was wont to journey abroad outside the confines of his kingdom, for his heart was restless and he yearned for the wide open pastures and dark forests of the west. Therefore, his realm being at peace, he brought together a caravan of counselors, warriors and merchants and had his asses saddled for a journey of many months. This having been accomplished, he left the affairs of the kingdom in the hands of Galen of Tondar, a trustworthy and true friend, and set off into the west to see what lay in the lands of the setting sun beyond the borders of his kingdom.

Many songs sing of that expedition of Anathar into the west, and how he first came to the region of the Cadarasians and found it a pleasant and rolling land, full of tall grasses and pastures, crossed with many rivers. He felt the wind from the Mountains of Bados swirling across the plains upon him and saw the richness of the soil there. It is told in other tales how he heard the songs of the nymphs singing in the forests and was smitten with desire to dwell in that land. Therefore the heart of the great king was moved with love for that region, and he compelled his companions to press further to the west, though they were sore tired and would have returned to Maruda. It was on the third day after entering the region of Cadarasia that Anathar first espied the horses of Elabaea, and the Elabaeans themselves. For as he stood poised on an elevated ridge, looking out across an expanse of grassland, he saw in the distance a herd of horses drinking at a low-laying creek. Near them he saw a party of men, though he was too far afield to descry anything else about them. He marveled at the beasts he saw, which looked somewhat like the donkeys of Maruda but with much greater majesty. Then he said to his companions, "Let us go down there and see what these marvelous beasts are, and what kind of men these are who tame them!" So they dismounted and approached the men on foot.

When he approached the creek, he hailed the men and bid them speak with him. The men marveled, for never before had they seen any man so glorious or powerful as Anathar. He towered above them, his raven black beard resting upon his mighty chest, from which issued his thundering voice. His robes were of finest silks, embroidered with gold and silver, and his royal helm was of glittering gold and fashioned in the manner of a falcon embracing the rising sun. In his hand was a great spear of ash, five cubits in length, with a head of shimmering bronze. His countenance seemed to be that of a god, and they trembled in fear of him as he spoke and would have fled had they not been so filled with terror.

But Anathar removed his helm and put forth his hands in friendship, and the men trusted him and put faith in Anathar. As they conversed, Anathar saw their speech was like unto the speech of Maruda, albeit with several diverse sayings and words, so that he perceived that they must be of similar stock as he. There by the creek was the first meeting between the Marudans and the men of Cadarasia, the herders and shepherds who peopled those fertile plains which Anathar admired. And Anathar inquired much concerning the horses, what they were, how the men used them, and how many there were. Anathar greatly marvelled to see the Cadarasians mounting the horses and riding them about the plains, and urged that they might sell some to him to take back to Maruda. Therefore, as it is told, Anathar purchased three horses from the Cadarasians, as well as a horsemaster to train the Marudans in the art of riding. Then Anathar parted from the horsemen with many words and tokens of friendship and promised to return again unto them. Thus did they part in amity, and thus was the horse first brought into Maruda.

It is not known where Anathar's eyes first fell upon the fair horses of Elabaea and the sturdy men of Cadaras, but it is said to be in the region of An Hered by the Brook of Cadar, and this is asserted by the people of Cadaras to this day.

But cruel fate had decreed a dire end for Anathar, for never again did he return to fair An Hered. He instead went into the north, where he was slain, gored to death by a fierce and fell boar, as is told in other tales. And the nymphs took his body and washed it and buried it in the woods near the source of the Sehu and Gihon rivers, and no one knows its location to this day. His mother, who was of the kin of the nymphs of that region, wept bitterly, and her lament is still sung of in the dirges of Maruda.

Nevertheless, the Marudans, also called men of Caeylon, continued to venture west into Elabaea (for that was what they called the region) and made alliances with many of the clans who lived there, especially the Cadarasians and their kin, the Asylians. The Marudans gave their sons and daughters in marriage to the Cadarasians and Asylians, and likewise they took the sons and daughters of Elabaea in marriage. Every spring the merchants of Maruda came to the city on the plains, Cadaras, and purchased from the people there a great deal of horses and feed, and greatly enriched that city. Likewise, the Marudans taught the Cadarasians and Asylians the art of smelting bronze into necklaces, jewelry, armor, and many fine things. For before this, the clans of Elabaea knew how to work bronze, but they used it only for sword blades, spears and shields, but did not possess the knowledge of making fine things. The Marudans also gave to the Elabaeans much of their skill in building and architecture. Thus friendship grew between the two peoples, and many more Marudans began venturing into Cadarasia and Asylia. Their ties of kinship were strengthened because Maruda was at war with Epidyimia to the north, that great kingdom which also often assailed the Cadarasians and Asylians and put them to rout. So the two peoples were also allied in their loathing of the Epidymians. For generations there was free concourse between Asylia and Caeylon, and though few Cadarasians went there, many Marudans came into the west, and some built towns and villages therein.

But it soon came to pass that the Marudans learned the ways of war, and this was not entirely their fault, for they were oft assailed at home by foes without, and the Zhinkanthans oppressed them sorely for many years. But once the men of Maruda had learned war, they loved it more than commerce and began to demand more horses from the people of Cadarasia. Every year the Marudan merchants from Caeylon returned to Cadarasia and asked for ever greater amounts of horses, for the kings of Caeylon desired that their armies should be the most powerful in the world and that every soldier should be born aloft on horseback. They had attempted to sire the horses of Elabaea back in Maruda, but for reasons they knew not, the horses would not breed when taken to Caeylon. Thus, they returned year after year to purchase more. Furthermore, many of the enemies of Maruda had begun coming to Cadarasia and buying horses as well, so that each spring there were always too few steeds available to meet the demand of the Marudans. They also demanded many other things, like cattle, bronze, and many hundred wagonloads of timber from the fair trees of Cadarasia every year.

And the Marudans began to be wroth with the Cadarasians, and said, "You do us ill, men of the plains, in witholding your horses from us while at the same time selling them to our foes. Is this how you demonstrate your gratitude for the leniency of our lord Anathar, who gave unto you the kinship of Caeylon?" But the Cadarasians said, "Ever have we been amiable to your merchants! God knows we have taken them into our homes, sold them our finest stallions, and even given our daughters in marriage to them, to be taken off to the fiery land of Caeylon, an arid land of sand and sun which we have never seen. We swear before the gods, and by the beard of Manx, that no ill will do we bear thee." So the wrath of the Marudans was turned away, but they came nigh unto Cadarasia, even within sight of the city, and built themselves fortifications there, for the purpose of stopping all other peoples but themselves from coming to do trade with Cadaras.

In the one hundred and sixth year after Anathar died, it came to pass that Dathan came to the throne of Maruda, and he ruled Caeylon for twenty-nine years, during which he made life bitter for the Cadarasians, for he was a fierce king, and sought to impose tribute on Cadarasia and Asylia, which had ever been free and subject to no kingdom or ruler. And he exacted by force what had once been given freely as gifts, for he sought to wear down the Elabaeans and settle their land with Marudans, so as to take Cadarasia and Asylia and make them the westernmost marches of his domain. Therefore, he ringed Elabaea in with fortresses, so that no other people could enter that region (and to prevent the Elabaeans from entering into Caeylon). Then he imposed heavy taxes on the people there and sent many soldiers to the land to collect them. Therefore, the caravans of Maruda laden with silks and bronze artifacts were replaced by companies of soldiers and forests of whetted bronze spearheads glittering in the rising sun, marching from the east. The plains about Cadarasia and Asylia were littered with camps of Marudans, a great number of the horses of Cadarasia were seized by the Marudans, who gave in recompense only a pittance of what they had willingly paid before.

But Dathan found the Elabaeans to be hardy folk, for though they paid their tribute they showed no sign of weakening. On the contrary, many of them who had hitherto looked favorably upon the Marudans now became downcast and murmured in their homes by night. Therefore he grew wary of them and caused to be

10

built on the hillside east of Cadaras the great fortress of Danath Hered. Its walls were thick enough that two chariots could drive side by side upon them, and they were so tall that no arrow or spear could reach the battlements. Furthermore, they built the fortress so that it commanded the Brook of Cadar which fed the city with water, and thereby threatened to deprive the Cadarasians of water if they should not submit at all times to the demands of the men of Caeylon. And in those days many men of Caeylon went forth from Danath Hered and took for themselves women of the Cadarasians and the Asylians whom they found working or lingering in the fields. They took these women to wife and offered no payment in exchange for them to their fathers. Thus did the men of Caeylon make life exceedingly bitter for the peoples of Elabaea and despoil them of their daughters, and many a lovely maid of the fields and rills of Asylia passed away the years of their life under the stifling sun and dark eyes of their Caeylonic masters.

It came to pass when Dathan was advanced in age that his strength failed him and he found he could not get warm, though many blankets were laid upon him. This sickness lasted many months, and it so happened that one day as he was conducting business from his chamber, he caught the eye of the wife of one of his officers standing in the vestibule outside his chambers. He called the officer, and the officer said, "Here I am, lord." Dathan said, "Tell me, your wife looks different than the women of Maruda. Her hair is brown like the wheat at harvest time, not black like the women of our country; and her arms are white as ivory and lovely. Furthermore, she stands much taller than I am accustomed to see our women stand. From whence does she come?" Then the officer replied, "O live forever, great king! I obtained her from the people of Elabaea when I was in Cadarasia, for I was out near the town one day and saw her coming in from the fields. I was taken by her beauty and took her unto myself to be my wife. Furthermore, all the women there are of like appearance."

At this the heart of Dathan was moved with desire, and he called forth his servants and scribes and told them, "Send orders to the commanders and captains of the army who are dwelling at Danath Hered and tell them to take from the Cadarasians fifty of the most lovely young virgins they can find to be sent here to Maruda and serve me in my harem, for I am old and the chill of death is upon me, and I am desirous of the company of women, especially the beautiful maids of Elabaea." So the scribes transcribed the king's command, but when they had finished, he added, "And tell the captains to bring the most beautiful daugters from among the houses of the lords of Cadarasia and Asylia. These will be hostages towards the good will of the Elabaeans and will also serve in my harem."

So the decree went out, and the men of Maruda went forth from Danath Hered and began seizing the young virgins of the country to be sent back to Caeylon for the harem of King Dathan. But their comfort helped him not, and before the decree had yet been enacted for forty days, Dathan died and was buried in Caeylon in the tomb of his father Azuel. And he was succeeded by his son Belthazre.

Chapter 2
Of Belthazre and Eilia

It was the tradition among the Marudans that if their king promulgated a decree, that decree was revoked upon his death unless his successor should proclaim it still in force and seal the decree with his royal signet ring. When Dathan died, Belthazre, who was young and spirited, let fall the governing of the kingdom and gave himself to merrymaking with his friends, giving no thought to the affairs of Asylia and Cadarasia. And after the days of mourning for Dathan were complete, Belthazre proclaimed a festival throughout the city of Caeylon to last for forty days to celebrate his coronation. Never in the all the days of Maruda had such a feast been seen, for nobles from every corner of the kingdom came unto Caeylon and brought with them an abundance of wine, slave girls, colored tapestries, fools and an abundance of treasure with which to play games of chance and make merry with the young king. Belthazre himself declared a remission of taxes for the inhabitants of the city for the remainder of that year and spent lavish sums on decorating his palace for the festivities. He also gave a large sum to the Highpriest and the various cults of the city, that sacrifice should be offered continually to his health and long life. But of all the gods, most of all Belthazre was devoted to Mardu. Thus the people of Caeylon reveled and Belthazre gave no thought to the people of Elabaea and did not renew the decree of his father Dathan to take the virgins of that land. And for a time, no more young maidens were taken. So the men of Cadarasia and Asylia said to themselves, "The Marudans have repented from the evil which Dathan did to us; perhaps we will have peace." But the shadow of Danath Hered still fell heavy on Cadarasia.

It came to pass on the final night of the feasting that Belthazre was reclining at table with all of his princes and nobles, and with him was his wife, Narússa, a Kushite, whose skin was as olive and whose hair was as the night. As the evening drew on and their eyes grew heavy with wine, Belthazre called for his musicians to play for him in his court and minister to him. Now when they came before him and began to play on the harp and lyre, the flute and the drum, he noticed that the girl who played the flute was of fair skin, not dark skinned like his wife Narússa. Furthermore, he noticed that her hair was flaxen and yellow and fell lightly upon her shoulders, not black and heavy, as was the hair of his wife Narússa. Furthermore, he noticed that her eyes were emerald green and her lips full and red. As he listened to her flute playing, he was filled with desire, and he called a halt to the music and summoned the girl before him, saying to her, "Girl, tremble not, for no harm will befall you at my table. Though I am king of a mighty land and though I have taken life in war with spear and sword, it is rightly said that I am benevolent and gentle to those who esteem me. Is it not so?" Then all the lords said, "Yea lord, it is so." Then Belthazre said, "Therefore, tell me your name, fair maid, and the land of your birth."

Then, looking to the floor and not daring to lift her eyes to the kingly presence, she said, "My lord, my name is Eilia, and fair Asylia is my home, far westward beyond the scorching sands, in the pleasant meadowland between Erriad and Cadar where the rills of the Gihon drain off into the fields of Elabaea, making them fertile and soft. When I was but a youth I was seized by the men of Maruda while I tended my father's flocks in the fields (for in our land it is custom that the eldest daughter tend the flocks while the eldest sons win glory in the hunt). I was espied from afar by a Marudan captain, as Anathar espied the horses of Elabaea long ago. The captain swept down upon me; with great force he overtook me and bore me away. He brought me hither, away from my land and here sold me to a traveling troupe for the sum of ten pieces of silver. Henceforth I have played flute in this troupe for my master."

Belthazre gazed upon her white arms and proud neck and was filled with wonder, for he had spent his youth making war in the east and knew very little of the people of the west, for he had never been there. Then he said to Eilia, "Gaze at the floor no longer, maiden of the west, for this day shall be accounted blessed by thee. I myself will ransom thee and pay any price your master shall demand, even up to one hundred gold pieces. Go, fetch him at once and tell him that the king would speak with him concerning this." He said this part because he was filled with desire for Eilia and wished to take her to wife, but also because he was drunk with much wine.

At this his wife, dark-eyed Narússa, took great offense and furled her brow against Eilia. Then the queen said, "Great king, let business be postponed until the bright rays of Shamash grace the morning! Night is for merriment, and more so since this is the last day of your celebration!" Belthazre smiled at Narússa and said, "Do you fear the toppling of your throne, wife of my youth? I say, put such thoughts away, thou foolish and simple-minded woman!" Then to his lords he said, "But nevertheless, that our feasting be not soured by the evil eye of my wife, let it be as she says. We will postpone this affair until morning." Therefore he sent Eilia away with many gifts and promised to call for her again on the morrow.

But after the music fell silent and the king's eyes grew heavy, Narússa left his presence and went with haste to the captain of the palace guard. She said to him. "Captain!" And he said, "Here is your servant." Then she told him, "A young woman of Asylia has just now been dismissed from the king's presence. She is traveling with a group of musicians out of the palace. Overtake her upon the causeway and slay her." But the captain trembled and said, "O great queen, how is it that you command me to do such a thing? Shall I murder an unarmed woman in dark of night? For if I obey, I shall sin against heaven and against the goddess Innana, to whom women are especially dear. Yet if I disobey, you shall accuse your servant of treason and have me put to death!" Dark-eyed Narússa said to him, "Gird up your loins like a man and have no fear! I would not have commanded her death if she were not treacherous, and is not your duty to protect the king's person? Therefore, cease thy trembling and womanly quaking and do your duty! But to further persuade you, I shall give you twenty pieces of silver, as surety that this shall be done." Then she gave the captain a pouch of silver, equal to six month's pay. So he strengthened himself and said, "O great queen, it shall be done as you command!" Narússa therefore retired to her chamber, content that the king should never again be dazzled by the emerald eyes and flaxen hair of Eilia.

So the captain took three men and overtook Eilia and her troupe as they made their way out of the palace on the causeway. He hailed them as if to stop them for some trivial matter, but when he approached with his men they drew their swords and slew Eilia there upon the causeway, midway between the inner gates of the palace and the garden gate. The other players in the troupe the captain slew also. Thus did Eilia the Asylian perish in blood in fierce Caeylon, far from the friendly fields and rills of Asylia, of which many songs have been written. The most famous, translated into the common tongue, says:

15

She soothed the king with her gentle flute,
but perished for it by cruel bronze.
Her hair fell like gold and held the king enraptured,
but her blood spilled out and sullied the lustre of his royal court.
Her green eyes stopped the heart of the master of the Maruda,
but her flesh knew the warmth of day ne'er again.

Now another song tells how after this, the captain repented of his deed and made atonement by giving the twenty pieces of silver to the priests of the Temple of Innana in Kush, but that does not come into this tale.

When morning came, King Belthazre was told, "The Asylian woman Eilia whom you wished to take to wife has been found slain on the causeway outside the palace." Then Belthazre was exceedingly wroth, so much so that he trembled with anger, and he commanded all his officers and ministers to come before him in council. Then he summoned his wife Narússa to appear before him, and when she came into his presence, he thundered: "You brown-eyed sorceress! You witch, and daughter of a witch! Cursed be the day I layed eyes upon you in the red city of Kush! Cursed be the day when I, seeking refreshment for myself and my steed, came upon the clear fountain of Dar-bahir in the center of your fair city and saw you there batting your eyes at me!" Narússa trembled and bowed her head to the floor and said, "If my lord is wroth with me, let him speak his mind." Then Belthazre said, "Is there any man in Caeylon, nay in all Maruda, who does not know that the king is supreme? If any other man had dared to do what you have done, I would have brought him down to his grave in blood and hung his corpse from the gates of the city! But this I have against you: that you, by your womanly deceits, first put off my plans to seize the Asylian woman and then had her slain to deprive me of my joy! Does your conceit know no bounds, or is not even the king safe from the wiles of thy envy? Speak! Do you deny you have done this thing of which you stand accused?" Dark-eyed Narússa, her head to the ground, her raven black hair falling over her neck of iron, responded, "I do not deny it, lord. It is as you say."

Then Belthazre, frowning, called for his royal crown and diadem, the crown worn by Anathar, lost to Nammtar in the days when the Zhinkanthans held Morgyon in captivity, and then ransomed again in the days of Morgyon's ascendance. The crown and diadem were placed upon his brow, atop his black locks, his hair fresh and dripping with oil. Then he called for his royal robes, beautiful silken robes embroidered with gold and images of various birds and beasts, and donned them. Then he called for his battle spear and his scepter. The spear was brought to him, a hard, ashen beam tipped with flesh-cutting bronze, and the mighty king grasped it in his right hand, his hand callused from much war. In his left he was given the ancient scepter of the house of Anathar, by which decrees were promulgated, and by which the lives of men could be made or undone. Then he stood up, and when he did all his ministers and officers and attendants fell to the floor and prostrated themselves. As he stood, the sun rose in Maruda, and the temples around the city greeted the coming of the sun god Shamash with bells and chants, and the rays thereof fell through the window of Belthazre's chamber and lighted upon him, illumining his diadem and glittering spearhead, refracting in a hundred directions the gold of his robes. It was said thereafter that never had a king since Anathar been seen so radiant and splendid. And all the people cried out with one voice, "Mardu reigns in Belthazre! The god reigns and he speaks!"

Then Belthazre extended his royal scepter and said, "As I speak, let it be done! This I decree: You, Narússa, through your wickedness thought to deprive me of the delight of my eyes, the fair maid Eilia of far-off Asylia, and you did indeed best me in this. But my will shall be done, and none shall thwart me. This I say to you: I will indeed have a maid of Asylia to take to wife, whatsoever you may say of it! By the gods, before yesterday, I had a mind to leave the Elabaeans alone and to rescind the harsh exactions of my father Dathan upon them. But now it shall not be so! This is my command: that the order of my father Dathan be renewed and enforced which commanded all of the most beautiful daughters of the lords of Asylia and Cadarasia to be brought to Caeylon for the king's harem. And that the most beautiful of all of these shall take her place as my wife, equal to thee. Furthermore, let it be written, that if the Queen Narússa shall in any way try to hinder my will or do ill to the Asylian maids when they arrive hither, know that she shall suffer this penalty: she shall have her arms and legs hewn off and her body shall be thrown into the streets of Caeylon to be run over by a hundred chariots, according to Marudan tradition. Let all the world know this shall assuredly be!"

Then the ministers, officers and servants of the king all stood upright and shouted: "Yea, even so! Lord, even so!" Then Narússa was taken out of the king's presence and retired to her chambers, still quaking for her life. When Belthazre had affixed the signet of his ring to copies of his proclamation, he called to him his old friend Arahaz, a captain of the cavalry who had spent many years in Asylia and knew its land and its people well. Then Belthazre said, "Arahaz, you know the land of Elabaea more than any other man. Tell me, who among the daughters of the lords of that land excels most in beauty and grace?" Then Arahaz said, "Live forever, great king! The maid you seek is undoubtedly Osseia, the daughter of the lord Ioclus, who rules fair Asylia far beyond the Erriad at the foot of the highlands of Cyria. His house is the most renowned of all the houses of Asylia, for they say he descended from a god who dwelt in that region in ages past."

Belthazre said, "I care not for Asylian fables, only that I may possess a woman of exceedingly great beauty, so as to arouse that ghoul Narússa to envy. By god, I will light a fire in her bones that will not be extinguished for a hundred centuries, though the name of Belthazre utterly perish from the earth and the city of Caeylon and the great Temple of En'Thoth be covered by the desert sands unto the ending of the world! Therefore, see to it that my decree is sent forth into Asylia, and go there quickly and bring to me the maiden Osseia, daughter of Ioclus, along with the daughters of all the chiefs and lords of Asylia and Cadarasia, that they may be held as hostages here in Caeylon to serve at my pleasure, and against any possible attack from the Elabaeans, as my father Dathan decreed. Go then, and take your leave of the city within a fortnight." And Arahaz bowed low and said, "As the god lives, it shall be done." This then was the manner in which Belthazre turned his mind from feasting to covetousness and to bitter warfare.

Chapter 3
The Counsels of Ioclus

Now Ioclus was lord of the Asylians, the westernmost of the people of Elabaea, who dwelt to the north and west of the Cadarasians and occupied all of the plains from the Erriad-by-Sehu westward to the ascent to the Cyrian Highlands. It was in the shadow of the highlands that they had their city, Asylia, and from there Ioclus extended his rule. Since Asylia was further west than Cadarasia, the people there were less under the power of the Marudans and thus resented their presence all the more and were more wont to grumble against the men of Maruda than those of Cadaras who dwelt in the shadow of Danath Hered.

Ioclus was mighty among the men of Asylia, for according to their reckoning he was descended from the god Manx. This was what was told in the genealogy of Ioclus: how in ages past there had been a certain maiden, whose name was Orianna. This Orianna was exceedingly beautiful, the fairest and loveliest of all the daughters of Elabaea. She dwelt in the extreme northern marches of Asylia, near Epidymia, in the house of her father. One day while she was out keeping the flocks of her father in the noon sun, she reclined under a cedar and began to sing. Her song wafted on the winds to the north, where hoary headed Manx heard her from his mountain abode. He stepped forth and looked down upon the plain, and espied Orianna singing, and his immortal heart was smitten with longing for the girl. So he stroked his grizzled beard and gave a great cry, and the winds flew forth from his mountain and took up Orianna in a cloud, bringing her to the feet of Manx. There, upon the top of Mount Eriar, he took her to wife. However, after she had dwelt with him for some time, he said, "Orianna, it is not meet that mortals should dwell with immortals, or that flesh and blood should cohabit with divinity. Therefore I am sending you back to the house of your father, who has wondered at your absence these past three months. But do not fear, for you are now with child, and shall bear a son who will be mighty among your people, for he bears within him godsblood. And I will bless your house and look after it, unto the seventh generation." Then Manx stroked his grizzled beard and called for the winds, and they bore Orianna back to the cedars of her father's land.

Orianna gave birth to a son, Orix, and Orix took to wife Liala of Giha, and she bore to him Andor and Masoss. Andor begat Ancyrus, and Ancyrus took to wife Messinia and begat three sons: Ioclus, Naross and Arrax, who was deadly with the spear. Ioclus, being the eldest, was the lord of Asylia, and he took to wife Grianne of Cadarasia, sister of Garba, the lord of that city. To Grianne and Ioclus were born three sons, Masaros, Menelor and Eleth, and also three daughters, Osseia, the eldest, Saraeth, who was lame in the feet, and the youngest of all their children, blessed Manaeth, who is called Manissa. But of all the maids of fertile Asylia, light-footed Osseia, eldest daughter of Ioclus, was the fairest of all. Her almond-shaped eyes were of brown, and her hair the color of the myrtle in the fall. Her arms were delicate and smooth, and her flesh like alabaster. The men of Asylia said that never could one gaze upon her countenance and forget it afterward, and her face beamed with radiance that the elders said was derived from her divine ancestry. Many men had come asking her hand from Ioclus her father, but she had rebuffed them all. Gentle and kind, Osseia was the pride of the house of Ioclus, and the house of Ioclus was the boast of Asylia. Thus was the house of Ioclus.

When, therefore, Ioclus heard the decree of Belthazre, that Osseia was to be brought to Danath Hered to be turned over to the guard there and escorted hence to Caeylon in Maruda, he sent her away into the wilderness with his flocks for a fortnight until he should consider what course of action he ought to take. Nor would this seem unusual or unbecoming, since it was tradition in Asylia that the eldest daughters take the flocks out to pasture. Therefore, he sent her and her nursemaid, Neela, south of Asylia into the wild pastureland of Enna, about three days journey from the realm of the Lugarians. There she kept watch over the flocks of Ioclus, two hundred thirty choice sheep and many rams, and let them graze in the grassy heather of windswept Enna's plains. And at midday, when the sheep took their rest in the nooks and hillocks of the land to escape the weariness of the sun, Osseia would recline beneath the terebinth tree at En Ganar and sing the lays of Asylia in the shade of the noon whilst Neela, her nursemaid, took her rest.

It was on such a day, while Osseia and Neela were reclining beneath the great terebinth of En Ganar, that the sister of Osseia, Manaeth (who is called Manissa) came unto her in the wilderness, and with them was their brother Eleth, the youngest of the sons of

Ioclus. Manaeth was seated upon her ebony charger, Ruah, and with her Eleth came upon his steed. When they came upon Osseia under the terebinth tree, she was singing a lamentation for her maidenhood. Then Manaeth dismounted and called out, "Hail, fairest sister! The sun is high and the land is refreshed in the rest of noontide. Why then do you fill the air with your baleful dirges, your songs of woe?"

Osseia replied, "How is it that you ask me why I sing so sadly? You know the decree of the King of Maruda as well as I! A shadow hangs over me, dear sister, which no sunlight nor sweet song can dispel. For I behold my doom clearly, and the decree of Belthazre has brought weakness to my limbs and fear to my heart. Therefore, I am consumed with grief, and I sing to lament my end. Why does cruel fate thus taunt me, that I should be taken away from my home so young, never to know the love of a man, or see the rule of our brothers in the hall of Orix in Asylia? That I should never know the joy of children and children's children upon my knee, or rest in sweet death in the dark soil of my native land? I tell thee, I will suffer death before I suffer it to be so."

Manaeth said, "Perhaps you can yet have cheer, dear sister, for nothing is decided. You know not what lies ahead for you or our house." Osseia said, "But I know what lies ahead for me! Yes, a long journey across an arid waste devoid of friend or kin, to the hulking stone city in the midst of the burning desert! And to be taken unto the chambers of the king who lays waste to our land and grinds up the lives of our people, then to be shut away in the palace at the mercy of foul eunuchs and vain women, forbidden to set foot outside of it or ever tread on the wild grasses of my homeland again or hear the sounds of the rills which flow down from Gihon and Sehu in the spring! Yea, forbidden even to go where I will, until I waste away with age and am cast forth as a useless hag! This, sister, is why I lament so mournfully this day and every day until I meet my cruel fate."

Manaeth comforted her, and said, "Sister, you mustn't speak so! Are you not the eldest daughter of Ioclus, lord of the Asylians? If our mighty father should resolve to hold you against the will of the Caeylonic king, then all of Asylia and Cadarasia will rise in your defense, and not even Manx himself could pluck you out of this land, though you were twice as beautiful as Orianna!" But Osseia frowned and said, "Then I am doubly cursed, for either I go away to Caeylon and to my doom, or if I remain (as you say), the land will be drenched with blood on account of me!" So she brooded over her fate.

Then her brother, Eleth, said, "At least hold thy mourning until judgment has been passed by our father. Even now as we speak he has summoned together all the lords of Asylia and the lord of Cadaras, and they are in council as to what is to be done. It may yet be that a way out may make itself known to us."

Even as Osseia was dwelling in the wilderness and being comforted by Manaeth and Eleth, Ioclus had been taking counsel in the Hall of Orix in Asylia regarding Belthazre's command that Osseia be sent to Caeylon at once. Before him stood the six greatest lords of the Asylians, summoned from all corners of their lands: there was clear-headed Naross, brother of Ioclus and of all men most skilled at laying plans and stratagems; then there stood bold Arrax, younger brother of Ioclus, lord of Paros and renowned for his strength with spear and sword, of whom it was said that in the days of his youth he could hurl a spear through the trunk of an oak; also summoned were Amyntas of Kerion, a young and lordly warrior, both wise and strong, and Gygas son of the lord of Gela, and Hadrior, the son-in-law of Ioclus who was united in marriage to Saraeth, second daughter of Ioclus, who was lame in the feet. Hadrior was sullen and quiet, but of all men he was the most cunning with words and figures of speech. Also attendant upon Ioclus was mighty Garba, lord of Cadaras, who was the brother of Ioclus' wife, Grianne (who had died) and was equal in honor with Ioclus among the Elabaeans. Thus were the seven lords of the Elabaeans. Also present were the two elder sons of Iolcus, Masaros and Menelor, though they were forbidden from giving counsel in the deliberations because of their youth.

At that time, the lords of Asylia were locked in fierce debate and there was no agreement among them. They had spent the better part of the evening discussing stratagems and plans, but none of them seemed good to Ioclus, and the old king was wrapped in a cloud of doubt and indecision. Then Garba, mighty lord of Cadaras and brother-in-law of Ioclus, spoke up and said, "My kinsman Ioclus, is there any doubt as to what path lies before us? It will do us no good to reason with Belthazre, for he is an impulsive man and will only be brought to wrath by our petitions. Nor can we hide Osseia in the wilderness forever, a course which would only bring the Caeylonics to anger and sadness to ourselves and to your fair daughter. The only course that presents itself to me

22

is that we make bold and engage the Marudans in open war, fierce though they be."

Then Arrax, lord of Paros and youngest brother of Ioclus said, "Garba speaks true. The men of Maruda care not for our traditions or our people. Since the time of Dathan, father of their present king, they have known nothing but warfare and oppression. Might is the only counsel they will hear, and blood the only thing that will move their stony hearts. Therefore, let us mass our people and make war upon them quickly. Perhaps we can deal them a blow from which they will not recover and they may withdraw from our lands." Garba and the sons of Ioclus murmured assent to Arrax's words and clashed their spears and shields.

Then Naross, brother of Ioclus and wisest among men arose and silenced the assembly. Then he said, "Cool thy nerves, bold Arrax, for not everybody's spear is as hot for blood as yours. For a young man of great strength eager to win glory; to him is war valorous, and quick is that man's temper to grasp the spear instead of the hand. But what of the women who will no doubt suffer outrages at the hands of the men of Caeylon? What of the old who will be exposed to starvation and destitution, or the suckling infants, so fresh in the world yet who will only have a merciless rock and the dashing of brains to hope for? What of those whose throw is not as sure as yours or whose arm is not as strong and who will expose their bodies to wounding and maiming because of what you say rashly now? Brethren, if we must go to war, then so be it. But let us not commit to a course of action which may prove disastrous to our cause if by allowing cooler heads to prevail we may yet stave off destruction." Then all the assembly was quiet and Arrax was speechless.

Ioclus stroked his whitened beard and said, "Brothers both to me are bold Arrax and wise Naross and their counsel I take to heart, but it is the words of Naross which speak more true to me. Come, O wisest and most valorous of Asylia, is there no other honorable course left than to make war on Caeylon, on a mighty nation which has never known defeat or ceded the day to a rival?"

The Hadrior, the son-in-law of Ioclus rose and addressed the assembly and said, "Perhaps the time has come to consider that which has been in the minds of us all but which we have been loathe to speak: that the most prudent course of action may be to hand Osseia over to Belthazre. For whether we hide her or endeavor to make war, which would be folly, Belthazre will be wroth with us and will seek to chastise us, so we suffer either way. Is it right that the whole people should suffer because of one woman? Therefore, I say let her be turned over to Caeylon, though it rend our very hearts to do so."

Hadrior's statement caused a great clamor in the hall, and Amyntas, lord of Kerion, spoke harshly with Hadrior and said: "Thy treachery leaves bitterness in my mouth! Who are you to say such things of the daughter of our leige-lord, the fairest of all women, of whom it is said that the very likeness of Orianna of blessed memory is seen? A fine friend of the house of Ioclus you are, who would wed the middle-daughter of your lord but petition to have his eldest sent away to captivity!" And everyone else denounced Hadrior as well, not only for his counsel, but because he was husband of Saraeth, middle daughter of Ioclus. Now, Saraeth was very beautiful, but she was lame in the feet, for she had been dropped as an infant. Had she not been lame, Hadrior would have not been noble enough to wed her, but since she was lame and limped, her father Ioclus saw fit to give her to a lesser man. Therefore, Hadrior was not accepted by all the lords of Asylia as equal with them.

Then Gygas of Gela spoke up and said, "Like you all, I too abhor the words of Hadrior. But his words bring to mind another possibility that has yet to be considered. Suppose we give Osseia in marriage to one of the other young lords of Asylia? Then we can plead that she is already the wife of another, and that it would not be fitting or honorable to give her to another. Furthermore, Belthazre will not desire her if she is no longer a virgin."

Now, though Gygas proposed giving Osseia to another Asylian, his words provoked more of an outcry than those of Hadrior, because he had dared to mention her virginity in the assembly, and in front of her father no less. Therefore he was shouted down as well. But Ioclus said, "Peace, brethren. Were this any other day and any other matter, we would be right to blame Gygas for bringing up the matter of my daughter's virginity before my judgment seat in my own hall. By our customs, such a man is not blameless who does so, and Gygas would have to make restitution to me or else give me satisfaction in combat. But the times are evil, and though Gygas has spoken recklessly, it behooves us to at least consider what he says."

Then Naross said, "It seems to me, my lord, that Gygas' plan will doom us to ruin. Belthazre knows that Osseia is unmarried, for such a reason does he covet her. If we were to quickly marry her off, even be it to some noble lord, the insult of it would not be lost on the king, and he perhaps would be roused to punish us, no doubt by the slaying of whatever ill-fated man we wed Osseia to. Therefore, to do as Gygas says would be an open summons for Belthazre to chastise us for what he can only perceive as arrogant affrontery. Furthermore, even though Osseia were married, is this any surety that Belthazre will not seize her anyway? For the King of Caeylon reigns as master of the world and his will is always carried out. In our own tales, we tell of how the god Manx looked down from snowy Mount Eriar upon Orianna and seized her without regard to her father's house or to her maidenhood. If we assert such things of our gods, shall we presume a mere man to be any more virtuous? Gygas' proposal exposes us all to the same dangers as open war but gives us no security." Then Naross was seated and the hall was silent.

Then noble Amyntas rose, looking lordly and handsome in the torchlight, his locks bedewed with the wetness of the night shimmering upon his broad shoulders. He grasped his spear and said, "Brethren, it is plain to me that whatever path we choose we will suffer. Let us not seek to escape the road that Fate has laid out for us, for suffering will certainly come. Therefore, our question ought to be not how can we escape wrath, but rather which course is more honorable? For it is better to suffer greatly in the cause of virtue than to prosper in shame." Then all the lords cried "Yea" and clashed their spears against their shields.

Then Ioclus said, "Then, my noble brethren, it seems we only need to determine which course is the most honorable and our choice will be decided." Then the assembly cried with one voice, "We will bind ourselves to the will of Ioclus, in life or death." Then Ioclus continued, saying, "I am the eldest of three brothers, Naross coming after me and then Arrax. Naross has been gifted with wisdom, greater than any other among us, and Arrax with strength and prowess of war. They each outdo me in these. Yet I was given a measure of each, wisdom to rule, and strength to defend my claims and my people. I, too, was a warrior before old age bowed me low. In my youth, I brought down in one day seven Epidymians, brothers all, with my own spear. They thought to unhorse me, the fools! But I sent them down to the dust in blood and brought woe to the house of their mother that day. She looked for signs of their coming. She said to the runners, "What of my sons?" But she was brought to grief, and her gray hairs came down to the grave in mourning. And thereafter I was brought to the kingship in the days when my great lord and father Ancyrus went to his forefathers. Ever must the king choose wisely between fair words and fell deeds, between extending the hand and thrusting the spear. But it seems to me that all other courses are futile, and that if we are to maintain our honor and not be remembered as lords who brought shame and ruin to Asylia then we have no other path to take than the dark way of blood."

Then cool-headed Naross said, "Brother, you admit plainly that I exceed you in wisdom. Hear me then! I know and declare that we cannot win this war. The men of Caeylon cannot be brought down. We may slay some of them by ambuscade or by night raids, but their men are greater than ours in numbers and in the power of their chariots. In choosing war, we may die gloriously, but die we must in the end."

But hot-blooded Arrax replied to his brother, "Shall fear of death stop us? Have we not all vowed to follow the advice of Amyntas and take our stand upon our honor? Though I defer to Naross as my elder brother and as much more knowledgeable, I must ask why should we to grant the Caeylonics victory before the battle has even begun? Who says they cannot be defeated? Is it not written in their own annals that in ages past, when those who had known Anathar were still alive, that the men of Zhinkanthas came upon Maruda unawares and slew many of them and even took their king, Morgyon son of Anathar, as a hostage? The Marudans prevailed in the end, it is true, but not before the men of Zhinkanthas dealt them a mighty blow that almost sent their kingdom into ruin. Are we not as bold and courageous as they?"

Then Garba said, "Whether in victory or death, we shall at least make known to the men of Caeylon that Asylia and Cadarasia are not to be trampled upon. If they think to stomp us, we shall prick their feet sorely!" Then all the assembly laughed at this.

Ioclus silenced them, stood upright and held aloft his spear, by which was meant that he was to render judgment. "I resolve to send the lady Osseia away, far to the north, to Cyrenaica on the coast, far from the reach of Belthazre. There, in a place where Marudan eye has never seen, Osseia will remain safe. This shall anger Belthazre and put my whole house in danger, and therefore, we shall go as well, at least as far as oaks of Lissus south of Thon and the land of the Iturs. There we shall part ways, Osseia going

26

north to Cyrenaica, and myself and my house taking to the wilderness."

Garba was indignant and cried out, "Then your plan is to flee and leave Cadaras to bear the brunt of Caeylon's fury alone? Have you forgotten the great fortress of Danath Hered which lies so close to my city that at dusk the shadow of their keep falls upon our gates?"

Ioclus said, "Peace, Garba. Though my wife Grianne, your sister, perished long ago, still we are united by many bonds, and I would not leave you to face Maruda alone. Nay, we shall not spend our time in the wilderness hiding but shall traverse the land hither and thither, from rugged Ituria and Cyrenaica westward to the Cyrian Highlands and the dreadful woods, planted by the titan Agenor in ages past. We shall muster allies from the battle-hardened Lugarians and the fierce Moguls in the south and the bands of hillmen who spread themselves out upon the rugged foothills of Bados. Perhaps we shall even make amends with the men of Epidymia, all of whom are mighty, and draw them in on our side. When we have gathered allies, we will come to your aid in Cadaras and overthrow Danath Hered."

Then Gygas said, "My lord, this plan is madness! By drawing the other peoples of Elabaea into this folly, you invite the Marudans even further into our land and draw cold death upon us all!" But he was shouted down.

Then Ioclus said, "I am resolved in this course of action, Gygas. Therefore, hear my words: Menelor, Masaros, sons of my loins! Come hither! Fetch Eleth and thy sisters, Osseia, Manaeth and Saraeth. We shall all take Osseia north to the fair city of Cyrenaica upon the northernmost shores, where the mapmakers of Caeylon have never seen. Manaeth will accompany her in this exile, and Saraeth will go as far as Thon, to console her sisters' tears; then

Gygas contemplates the betrayal of Ioclus in the dark pass of
Nimru.

*Then he rode a little further, and as he came to the dark pass of
Nimru in the foothills of the Bados and the darkness of night was at its
thickest, he said to himself, "Is it not better for one maiden to perish than
for the whole nation to suffer?"*

she shall return hither with her husband, Hadrior."

"And what of me, my lord?" said Hadrior. Ioclus answered, "You, son-in-law, shall remain in the Hall of Orix with my brothers, wise Naross and bold Arrax until Arahaz, servant of Belthazre, comes seeking Osseia. When he comes asking for her, you must detain him with words, keeping him here as long as you can in order that we might have time to put more distance between us, for I reason he shall be here within seven days time. We shall make for the north. Gygas and Amyntas, bold lords of the Asylians, noble in speech and war, you shall go to the south and the eastern countryside and raise the hue and cry that war is come upon our land against the swarthy Marudan. Call all men to arms. The lord Garba shall remain in Cadarasia and stall the men of Caeylon if possible. Then, at the next full moon, let all of us here attend to this course of action and gather again at the Stone of Cruachan, where in times past the Elabaeans have gathered to take counsel. Bring thither every weapon-bearing man you can muster. From thence we shall sally forth and make war upon the Marudans, and who knows what our end shall be?"

This advice seemed good to the lords of Asylia, and after drinking many droughts for the prospering of their labor and swearing oaths of fealty to Ioclus and one another, they each departed for their own realm under the darkness of night, the moon being hidden.

But Gygas, son of the lord of Gela, was bitter and downcast, for he had been twice shouted down by the assembly and bore his shame heavily upon him. Furthermore, he himself was in love with Osseia and had proposed marriage to her before, but was turned down. He had entertained the thought that perhaps by his suggestion in the council he could win Osseia's hand again, if not by love at least by necessity. As he rode eastward throughout the night and the coldness of the latter watches fell upon the murky lowlands between eastern Asylia and the northern marches of Gela, his bitterness grew, and he reasoned to himself, "The words of Ioclus are utter folly. Has the old man lost his wits? Can the scattered peoples of Asylia make war on mighty Caeylon? I have seen their columns drilling on the flatlands. I have seen the forest of a thousand glittering spears coming forth from Danath Hered. Their steps are calculated and their armor is heavy and new. They march all to a single drumbeat, and their chariots are fearsome in war, riding down all who stand against them. When they fire their arrows, the very sun is blotted out by their multitude, and they are merciless in victory, content not only with the death of their enemy but with the enslavement of wives and the slaughter of children. To follow Ioclus is to invite doom upon us all."

Then he rode a little further, and as he came to the dark pass of Nimru in the foothills of the Bados and the darkness of night was at its thickest, he said to himself, "Is it not better for one maiden to perish than for the whole nation to suffer, as Hadrior said?" Then he turned his steed and rode due eastward, changing his course. He did not stop but rode on through the rising of the dawn, when the pink sun burns the mist from the fields of Cadaras.

Chapter 4
The Wickedness of Gygas

As Iolcus had said, so it came to pass. For only a day after he and his kin departed from Asylia for the north, Arahaz and a detachment of soldiers from Danath Hered arrived in Asylia seeking Osseia. They had already gathered many maidens from other regions of Elabaea and now were seeking the beautiful daughter of Ioclus, whom Belthazre had commanded to bring that he might take her to wife for the spite of Narússa. When they arrived at Asylia and the noble Hall of Orix, they were received by Hadrior, Naross and Arrax, who greeted the men of Caeylon cordially. Then Arahaz showed them the royal decree of Belthazre and commanded that the maid Osseia be brought forth, but Naross said, "She has recently gone on progress with her father and his kin into the wilds of the west on a hunt and is not expected back until the next full moon."

This greatly angered Arahaz, and he perceived some treachery on the part of the Asylians and would have pursued the matter, but his captains said, "Lord Arahaz, we are strangers in this land and have no force with us suitable to make any campaign. Shall we pursue them into a wilderness we do not know, perhaps to be set upon by ambush and slaughtered? Let us rather return to Danath Hered and order the maid to appear thither within a fortnight. Then, if these wildmen persist in their duplicity, we can return hither with a sufficient force to teach them not to despise the commands of the King of Caeylon." This advice seemed good to Arahaz, and so he warned Naross and the kin of Ioclus, saying, "I perceive some deceit on your part, my lords. Yet I will return to where I came, but hear this: if the maid Osseia does not appear before me in Danath Hered within one fortnight, know that I will return here again, not in an entourage of emissaries bearing sealed parchments, but at the head of an innumerable host of the men of Maruda, bearing a sword thirsty for blood. And you shall all see how the king deals with those who are deceitful with him!" Then Arahaz went back to Danath Hered and did not pursue Ioclus into the wilderness.

But Ioclus, as he had determined, had gathered up his house and made north for the oaks of Lissus by Thon. With Ioclus were his three sons, Masaros, Menelor and Eleth, and his three daughters, Osseia, Saraeth and Manaeth. He also took with him four of the most trusted servants of his house, men who had served him long years since the time of his father Ancyrus. Also he took with him Neela, the maid and companion of Osseia his daughter, whose beauty was unrivaled among women.

Osseia was gentle and delicate, but noble, and bore the journey with grief and silence, being comforted by Saraeth her sister, who was above all most compassionate. But Manaeth, though she was beautiful, preferred to ride in the rear with her brothers, for she loved martial things and would have gone openly to war had it been the custom of her people. She was prudent and modest, but also beautiful, and her aim with the spear was sure, as she had been taught by her uncle Arrax when she was young. Her uncle, seeing her love of warfare and horsemanship, gave to her as a gift a marvelous black charger, named Ruah by Manaeth, which means "wind." Ruah was very dear to her, and it was said among the sons of Ioclus that Manaeth rode upon Ruah as skillfully as any man of Asylia.

When Ioclus and his house had ridden for five days with but a few hours rest, they halted by the great oaken slopes of Lissus, which border the land of Asylia on the north as one goes up towards the region of the Iturs, for they were very weary and saw a storm coming upon them. There they pitched their tents among the great oaks and rested themselves. Then Osseia sat down under the shade of the great branches and wept, and she was comforted by her sister Saraeth and her mistress Neela. She looked out upon the hillsides and said, "See, dear sister, a storm is rolling in upon the hillsides! Its dark clouds encompass them about, and soon rain and thunder shall break forth upon the land. The winds shall come and beat fiercely upon the trees and shrubs of the hillside, and some shall verily be torn forth and swept away, never to rest their roots in the cool earth of their native soil again. And yet who can stop it? Can the twig challenge the wind and say, 'What are you doing?' Can the hillside say to the storm, 'Take thy blustering fit someplace else and leave my trees be?' Assuredly, no. As sure as the storm will break forth upon these hills this very evening, so shall cruel Fate break upon me a torrent which will beat harshly on our land. Asylia, jewel of the earth, shall surely endure, but not before her most priceless sprout is torn there from and cast away to a place Manx himself could not descry." Then she wept and was comforted by Neela and Saraeth. And when her tears began to fall, so too did the heavens begin to loose their treasury of rain upon the earth.

But Gygas, who was bitter against Ioclus, had ridden without rest to Cadaras upon leaving the Hall of Orix. Upon reaching the city, he did not go up to it (lest he should see Garba or one of his house), but spent another day and went round about it, so that he approached it from the east, by way of Danath Hered and the road to Caeylon. When dusk came and the cover of shadow, he went up to the gates of the fortress and demanded an audience with Arahaz. Arahaz had just recently returned from his sojourn to Asylia and was in a foul mood, but he came to the courtyard and met Gygas nonetheless. Arahaz said to Gygas, "On what urgent business do you trouble me, ill-favored son of Elabaea?" Gygas did not trade words with him, but came out directly and said, "What will you give me if I deliver Ioclus and the maiden Osseia into your hands? For they have fled into the wilderness and are even now plotting war against Belthazre and the men of Maruda, and only I know where they are encamped."

When Arahaz heard this, his countenance lightened, and he grasped the shoulder of Gygas and said, "Forgive my harsh words, lord. I have just recently come in from the western wilds, and I know that the people of Ioclus are stubborn and hard of hearing. But you have wisdom in you! Tell me what you would have for your services to the king." Then Gygas brooded within himself and finally said, "In years past, I courted the hand of this very Osseia for whom you now seek, but was rebuffed by her. She is indeed the most beautiful in the land, and I envy the king's choice. Yet it is fitting that the choicest cut of meat is always reserved for the king's table, and so it is with women. Therefore, swear to me that when I have delivered the maiden Osseia into your hands and you have had your vengeance on Ioclus and his house that you will deliver to me Manaeth, the youngest daughter of Ioclus who is fair like her sister. Swear an oath that you will neither kill her nor send her away to the king's harem, or take her for yourself, but will give her to me in betrothal." This was the price demanded by Gygas.

Arahaz laughed and said, "Thy price is light as it is rendered in Caeylon. For you might have asked for jewels or slaves or wealth, or perhaps a palace in the Caeylonic marches! Yet you ask only for a woman." But Gygas said, "The price would not seem so light had you seen Manaeth's beauty, for the men of Asylia value a woman far above the men of Maruda, and in this we are superior."

But Arahaz said, "Watch your tongue when you presume to criticize our custom, lest I rip it from thy treacherous mouth! You shall have your Asylian wench, only see that you deliver Osseia and Ioclus to me." Then Arahaz took Gygas into the inner courts of Danath Hered and swore and oath by Mardu that Manaeth would be delivered up to Gygas in exchange for his betrayal. Then Gygas was lodged in the fortress and forbidden to leave. Two days hence, Arahaz assembled a company of picked men, forty whose aim with spear and arrow were deadly and whose sword arms were strong. Then he harnessed the fastest horses to his chariots and prepared to ride off west in pursuit of Ioclus, according to the instructions given him by Gygas. Arahaz himself donned his most valuable suit of armor, a splendid scale coat given him by Dathan, father of Belthazre, which was made entirely of bronze and shimmered in the morning sunlight. And he placed Gygas in the chariot beside him and told him, "If you attempt to beguile me, I will hurl you forth from here and run your body over until your bones are crushed and your blood fills the ruts of the road." Then they went forth from Danath Hered to seek Ioclus and Osseia.

Meanwhile, the house of Ioclus remained encamped at the oaks of Lissus, for the great storm that Osseia had descried upon the hills had moved over them and broke forth with great fury upon the camp of Ioclus, so that the roads were washed out and many trees felled by the fierceness of the storm. A full day had passed and the torrents had not ceased, and Ioclus and his kin remained in their tents while the rushing of the wind beat upon them. But the storm unnerved the horse of Manaeth, and Ruah was frightened and broke from his harness, running into the woods and the evening downpour. Manaeth was greatly upset by this and went out to pursue him. Her brother Eleth tried to dissuade her from leaving, but Manaeth said, "Ruah was a gift from our uncle Arrax, and no horse is like him either among the Asylians, Cadarasians or the Marudans. I must seek for him." Eleth responded, "At least take my spear in case you find yourself in any danger." Then Manaeth wrapped herself in a green cloak of wool, took the great spear of her brother Eleth and set off into the night. She told no one but Eleth that she departed, for she worried that her father would fear for her. Then she went forth into the wet wildlands to the west of Lissus seeking Ruah her steed.

But even as she left and darkness fell, Arahaz, Gygas and the men of Caeylon approached Lissus from the east. When they reached the highlands near Lissus they had to dismount from their chariots, for the roads were greatly washed out by the storm. The sky was already grey with clouds, and by dusk it was almost as dark as the night by reason of the tempest. Then Arahaz said, "Praised be the gods who this night have delivered our enemies to us and provided us with cover such as no men on earth could do! This wind and rain will enable us walk into their very midst and strike them before they hear us!" Then Gygas pointed out to Arahaz a large grove of oak trees about five hundred yards from them, near the top of a gentle slope of tall wild grass, and said, "That is the camp of Ioclus." Arahaz divided his men into groups of twenty and crept up the hillside, encircling the camp of Ioclus. But Manaeth had fled into the west seeking her charger, and was not within the camp.

As Arahaz spoke, so it was. The men of Maruda crept silently to the camp of the Asylians without their knowledge. Furthermore, since there was a great storm, and since they were so far removed into the wilderness, Ioclus had ordered all of his people to remain in their tents and had not posted a sentry. When Arahaz was within a bowshot of the camp he was prepared to give the sign to attack, but Gygas was seized with pangs of remorse and halted him, saying, "Let it not be so, my lord. Is it the way of Maruda to slay men in their sleep? Rather, call forth and announce yourself. Is the camp not surrounded? Ioclus is an honorable man and has ever dealt truly with the men of Caeylon. Perhaps if we give him warning, he will yield up the maid Osseia willingly." Arahaz said, "So, you betray your master with your left hand but seek to save his life with your right? You are like the tall grass of this slope, blown one way today, another tomorrow. Yet let it be as you say." Then Arahaz had the forty men surround the camp tightly, so that they stood almost shoulder to shoulder, their spears lowered and ready to slay. But Gygas removed himself behind a large oak tree, that his lord might not see him.

Then Arahaz called with a loud voice over the din of the storm, "You can cheat Fate no longer, Ioclus son of Ancyrus! The gods have delivered you to me out here in this desolate place, and there is nowhere you can flee to. Therefore, yield up Osseia or resign your life at my hands!"

When he had thus yelled, the sons of Ioclus awoke and were first to arms, rushing forth from their tents. Yet in the noise of the storm and in the darkness they did not perceive that they were encompassed all about, and when they ran forth brandishing their swords, they were pierced down in a row by the spears of the Marudans, almost at the door of their tent. They lay on the ground writhing, and their life ebbed away even as the rain fell and washed their blood down the hillside. Thus the mighty sons of Ioclus all fell without landing a stroke.

When Ioclus, his daughters and his servants came forth from their tents they wept at the sight of Masaros, Menelor and Eleth laying slain upon the ground. Then a fiery rage overtook Ioclus, and he took up the sword of Masaros his eldest and rushed upon Azar, one of Arahaz's captains, and slashed the blade across his throat so that his blood came pouring forth from his body as it crumpled. As Ioclus looked at the slain man he called out, "The time for words is past! To death and honor!" and he picked up the spear of Azar and hurled it at Arahaz, but the skillful Marudan dodged it, though it struck Oruah his driver in the breast, pinning him to an oak.

Then Arahaz cried out, "Slay them, but harm not the maid Osseia!" So the Marudans moved in. The four servants of Ioclus took up their spears to make a defense of the place, but they were too tightly pressed and could not throw them, so that they were pierced from the front and the rear with many wounds and fell defending their lord. But one of the servants, Aön, managed to crawl forth from the camp upon his belly after taking many wounds in the back and sides, for there was much noise and darkness, and the wind and rain still blew.

But in the darkness the men of Caeylon made no distinction between man and maid, and Neela, maiden of Osseia had a spear pinned through her back while she sought to flee. Lame-footed Saraeth, daughter of Ioclus and wife of Hadrior also was slain with many wounds. Ioclus alone remained of the men, but he raged fiercely, as a bear deprived of its cubs. With the sword he slew three of the men who came upon him, and then hurled his ashen spear against Tanaah, the other captain of Arahaz, hitting him squarely in the face, a crash of tooth and blood and bone that cut him off from the land of the living. He also took up the spear of a slain Marudan and threw again for Arahaz, this time striking him in the knee with a sorely painful wound. Arahaz howled in agony, and his men closed upon Ioclus until he had no space in which to wield his sword, and he was run through with many spears, so that blood came pouring from his mouth and belly. Collapsing upon the

36

wet dirt, Ioclus fell dead among many slain.

As Arahaz attempted to draw himself up and staunch his wound, he saw light-footed Osseia standing wet and alone in the grove of oaks by the bodies of her brothers. Then he said with great anger, "It is because of you that all this has come upon your house! It is for your sake that I have spent five nights following your trail in this desolate place, and because of you that I am now sorely wounded and will never again lead men into battle. For what? For my king to satisfy his grudge against his wife. Yet come with me now and make a quick end to this folly!" Osseia began to come forward, as if she meant to heed Arahaz and go with him, but when she drew near, she hurled herself upon the spearhead of one of the Marudan soldiers, so that the spear burst through her belly and came forth from her back, and her blood splashed upon the ground and mingled with that of the other dead. Thus perished gentle Osseia upon the cold, wet bronze of Caeylon.

This brought great fear and trembling upon Arahaz, for he feared what Belthazre would say when he heard that the maid he sought had been allowed to perish. Therefore he ordered his soldiers out with great haste to return to Danath Hered, and had himself carried back down the hillside. But Gygas came forth and confronted him, saying, "And what of Manaeth, my prize?" Arahaz looked at him with scorn and struck him on the cheek with the butt of his spear, saying, "Thou fool! Thou craven who betrayest thy lord and then hides when the deed is done! Go pick among the dead for your prize, for I no longer care now that the maiden Osseia is slain." Then after leaving a single horse for Gygas, he moved back down the slope with his men, leaving Gygas alone.

Now when Gygas heard that Osseia had been killed and that there were no survivors, he was bitter with remorse and wept loudly, and he moved among the bodies of the slain, lamenting his betrayal. But even as he wept, Manaeth returned from the woods where she had gone to seek her horse, Ruah, which she had found hiding in the valley. In coming upon the camp, she came upon the wounded servant Aön struggling on the ground, and he said to her, "Take heed, princess! Foul deeds have been done this night, and Gygas, son of the lord of Gela, has betrayed us to the Caeylonics in exchange for thy betrothal. I fear thy kin are all slain." When he had said this, he expired in death. So Manaeth crept forward to the camp and saw only Gygas alone among the bodies, wailing for his treachery. When he had wept for some time, he mounted his horse and would have departed, but Manaeth mounted her charger Ruah and clutched in her white-knuckles the great spear of Eleth, which her brother had given her when she went seeking her horse. Then she cried, "Cruacha!" and led mighty Ruah through the bush so that they came bursting out of the darkness upon the campsite. Gygas turned his steed to see what was upon him, but quick-armed Manaeth hurled the massive spear of her brother squarely at Gygas and struck him in the collarbone above the armor, piercing his flesh through to the other side. He crashed off of his horse with a great clamor, his face in the mud, his sword beside him useless.

Then Manaeth dismounted and stood over him, saying, "So, you have named me for the price of your treachery? Are you not happy to see me then? Am I as splendid as your lying dreams told you? Ah, the deceit of desire! You thought to take me home to wife, to bear children by me and keep your house in the shadow of Marudan tyranny! But instead I have crushed thy bones and severed thy veins, and your blood pours out even now upon the mud." But Gygas could not talk, though he gasped for air and life in the throes of death. Then Manaeth said, "Thy name shall go down in infamy, and thy body lie unburied. May the shades take thy soul!" As she said this, dark mist covered the eyes of Gygas and his spirit left him. So perished the traitor Gygas upon Lissus' muddy slopes.

Chapter 5
To the Hill of Cruachan

After she had slain Gygas, she ran to and fro amongst the bodies searching for any who might be alive, but found none. Then Manaeth was filled with great wrath and agony and cried out curses upon the Marudans by all the gods and powers of heaven. Then she took her spear and tightened her cloak about her, preparing to make off in pursuit of the Caeylonics, for she supposed that they had taken Osseia with them. But then she saw her sister dead upon the ground covered in much blood, her white evening gown still upon her, stained with mud and gore. When Manaeth saw this she dropped to her knees and wept bitterly, then cried out: "Alas! I am deprived of my entire house in a single night! Fairest sister, most beautiful among women and gentlest of all the house of Ioclus, had I been here at least I could have perished with thee! Alas that you should have been born for such an end as this! Woe that I ran forth into the night and left you to perish without seeing thy face one last time!" Manaeth wept bitterly.

Then Manaeth worked through the night and into the following day burying her kin in a shallow tomb atop the hill at the oak grove of Lissus. Those who were slain were the lord Ioclus, his three sons Masaros, Menelor and Eleth, his two daughters Osseia the fair and Saraeth (who was crippled), the nursemaid Neela, and the four servants which Ioclus had brought with him, eleven persons in all. These Manaeth buried among the oaks of Lissus. Then at dawn she performed the customary rites for the dead, for the souls of her kin. But the Caeylonic dead, the captains Araz and Tanaah, Oruah the driver of Arahaz, and three of the common soldiers she hurled down the hill to be food for the carrion. But Gygas she left untouched where he died, that his body might rot and moulder in the heat of the day.

When dawn had fully come and the storm abated, Manaeth went into her father's tent and brought forth his great shield, four layers of hide overlayed with beaten bronze and rimmed with delicate silver ornaments, and strapped it upon her back. Then she took for herself the great spear of her father. A massive spear it was, five cubits in length with a head of whetted bronze sharpened and thirsty for blood, made of the finest ash of Lugaria and its circumference that of a small tree. In the days of her father's youth the spear had been given to Ancyrus, the father of Ioclus by the sons of Dyans, lord of Epidymia, as a peace offering. It was said that nobody save Ioclus had the strength to bear the great weapon in battle, and when he was but a youth he bore the great spear up and went with his father Ancyrus to hunt the wild boar that roamed south of the Gihon. The beast was cornered in the marhsy rushes, and Ancryus the king pursued it in, but the beast turned and tore him so that he fell wounded. The picked men of Ancyrus pressed hard against the creature, but it was mad with rage and gored many of them with its tusks. Finally, Ioclus took up his great spear and went into the rushes. The boar charged him, the beast with its head low and its eyes enflamed, but noble Ioclus with youthful strength and nimble feet dodged his charge and hurled his massive spear at the beast, bringing it down in blood. It was carried back to Asylia in triumph, and that day Ioclus won the honor of even his father. As it was sung at the betrothals of Ioclus and Grianne:

Before the fell beast of Gihon leaping, Ioclus aimed his throw—
And brought the fearsome creature down in a single well-aimed blow.

It was this mighty spear which Manaeth claimed for her own. When she had taken the spear and shield of Ioclus, she gathered what remained of the camp's rations and wrapped her green cloak about her, and mounting Ruah her steed departed from that place of death back down the slopes toward the southwest. Thus began many days of traveling through the wilderness alone, which Manaeth spent in weeping and lamentation. She passed over hillocks and heather-clad hills, wildplaces which the Asylians avoid and that have no name, neither in the tongues of Lugaria nor Cadaras. Over stone and plain she passed, riding hard towards Cruachan, a place unknown to the men of Caeylon. The chill winds of autumn were upon her, blowing fiercely out of the west and the choppy seas that buffet the cliffs there. She slept in the open with neither tent nor blanket, having only her horse for warmth; neither did she eat, for her haste was great. After much riding, she became lost in the nameless wilds and began to suffer sorely from cold and thirst. On the third day after leaving Lissus, she came in the morning upon a shady place with many ferns and lichen covered rocks. There she found a crystal fountain issuing forth from the mossy rock and running cooly down into the moist vale about her. She let her horse Ruah graze and knelt before the icy fount, drinking until her thirst was slaked, and then for the first time took some food. Then, wearied with much travel and sadness, Manaeth collapsed onto a mossy bed and fell into a deep sleep.

It came to pass that after much slumber she was awakened suddenly at noontide by a presence. She leapt forth from the ferns and grasped the mighty spear of Ioclus, thinking the Marudans were upon her. But instead she beheld a marvelous sight. Behold! There stood the lordliest stag she had ever seen in all her days. His height was taller than that of a man, and his legs were terrible and powerful to behold. His coat of fur was glistening white, whiter than the perpetual snows upon the tops of Mount Eriar. Most glorious were the antlers of the creature, which spread out majestically over its mighty head and seemed to branch off endlessly into a multitude of horny points, like the very tree tops in their number and power. When the sun fell upon the stag, its coat glimmered brilliantly, so that the glade where Manaeth stood was covered with glistening spots of light. Thus Manaeth beheld the beast in wonder and silence.

The stag quenched its thirst at the fountain and then looked at Manaeth, and she was cut to the heart and exclaimed, "Most lordlike and glorious of all beasts of the forest! You look at me as though the very light of reason were in thy eyes! Never in all my days or the days of my father has one such as you been seen in these lands! Now you test me sorely, for I am torn: I am partly of mind to fall down upon the damp earth and adore you as one of the very gods themselves, but my valor and bravery would have me take up this mighty spear and bring you down, for never has such a trophy been seen either in the Hall of Orix or in any of the halls of Epidymia or Cadaras!" Yet she neither prostrated herself nor took up spear, but simply gazed at the creature.

By and by the stag suddenly left Manaeth and leapt away from her, bounding off through the ferny glade into the woods. And Manaeth straightaway felt within herself a great sadness, greater even than the grief at the death of her kin, and perceived that she seemed to have lost something and was left restless. She ran after the stag and cried, "Do not leave me, I pray thee!" But the stag left her, and she was desolate. Then she said, "Now that I have seen thee, I shall pant for thee everafter." Thus was ever restless to see it again.

After lingering there for a time she mounted Ruah and left that nameless glade, riding south into the wilderness, hoping to strike for the hill of Cruachan though uncertain of its exact location. After four days of riding, she entered into the broad and wild plains of southwest Asylia and saw the lofty hill of Cruachan towering over the landscape and draped in the shadow of the clouds. She pressed on, coming at length to the hill, and ascending it, to the very Rock of Cruachan, where Ioclus and the other lords of Asylia had agreed to gather at the next full moon. It was at this rock where ever and anon the kings of Asylia had been proclaimed and the direst judgments were rendered. There she collapsed with fatigue.

While Manaeth was traversing the desolate places, word had come to Belthazre in Caeylon that the mission of Arahaz had failed, and that not only Ioclus but Osseia, too, had been slain and Arahaz crippled by Ioclus' spear. Then Belthazre raged about his palace uttering curses and invectives against the barbarous Asylians and swore that he should yet have his revenge upon them. Then Narússa came before him and would have spoken, but he said, "Who summoned thee here, bearer of ill tidings and wicked counsel?" Narússa only smiled and said to the king, "Why is the king wroth at the loss of but one Asylian maiden? Did not your servants recently bring you an entire caravan of Asylian maidens from which to take thy pleasure?" But the king was wrathful with her and said, "Simple minded woman! True, when you deprived me of the Asylian Eilia by treachery, it grieved me sorely and I swore in my wrath to take to wife Osseia, daughter of Ioclus, lord of Asylia. Now so too has she perished and robbed me of my desires! But think not that this alone has made me downcast, or that I should be crestfallen over this for long. No, rather it is this truth: that in dying, Ioclus has dared to assail the men of Maruda, and my servants tell me that the torch of rebellion is being raised throughout Elabaea. The Asylians and Cadarasians are daring to challenge my might, and it is for this reason that I am wrathful."

Narússa remained silent for a time and then said, "And what shall the king's response to their challenge be?" Belthazre said, "Ioclus, though he be dead, can be forgiven for lifting hand against my warriors. Indeed, what father would not raise his spear in defense of his daughter? But he has paid for it in blood. None save the house of Ioclus has yet raised spear or sword against me. The rest of the people still go on as they always have. Shall I punish them all for the revolt of a single house? Therefore, I will bear out the days and see whether the intent of the Elabaeans is good or ill. Who knows? Perhaps they shall end this peaceably."

Then Narússa laughed and said, "Where is the might of Belthazre, son of Dathan? What has become of his reason? Were your father Dathan here, what would he say about the stratagem you now propose? Why wait for the Asylians and Cadarasians to unite the peoples of Elabaea against you? Strike them now whilst they are divided, for their lord has only recently been slain and their grief is still fresh. Send forth your legions! Lay waste Cadarasia, subdue proud Asylia and bring the Asylians hither to work in the mines and bear the burdens of the Marudans, who are rightful masters of the earth. Will you wait until they are strong and can mount a resistance? My lord, let it not be said that the King of Caeylon is tepid!"

Belthazre frowned and said, "Say no more about this, nor invoke my father, you envious serpent, eager for my own destruction! Much wealth comes from Asylia in trade and tribute. Shall I disrupt it because of your shrill-voiced speech?" Then dark-eyed Narússa said, "The servants who have come lately from Asylia say that even now the men of that region are gathering by moonlight to train with spear and arrow against Caeylonic arms. Be not a craven! Strike them sooner than later!" Then Belthazre became greatly enraged and said, "Get thee hence from my sight! If you come to see me again regarding this, I shall strike your head from your body! I will punish the Asylians in my own time; but when I have finished punishing them, I shall come and chastise you, you Kushite witch!" Narússa thus trembled and removed herself from the king's presence, but her words gnawed the mind of Belthazre and haunted him while he paced his torchlit halls by night.

The king knew not of Manaeth, who had survived the slaughter at Lissus, but thought the house of Ioclus extinct. Therefore he made no urgent move against Asylia, but turned the matter over in his mind for many days. By and by it came to pass that the next full moon arrived, the time appointed for the lords of Elabaea to gather at the rock of Cruachan and sally forth against the men of Caeylon. They had not heard news of Ioclus' journey, nor did they yet know of the death of all his house. Arrax was the first to arrive at the rock, bringing with him four hundred picked men from Paros and its environs, all dark-haired and in the vigor of youth, each bearing a bright bronze shield and a solid spear of hardwood tipped with flesh-ripping bronze. It was Arrax, uncle of Manaeth, who first saw her as he ascended the steep hillside of Cruachan. As he crested the top of the hill he beheld her layed out upon the ground, asleep with grief and weariness. It was Arrax that she saw first upon awakening, and to him that Manaeth delivered the news of what had befell Ioclus, Osseia, and their house in the wilderness. When Arrax heard it he tore his clothes, and all the company of Paros wailed aloud from the hill of Cruachan. As the men of Paros wept, the company of Naross and his band of Asylians were approaching from the east. And Naross said, "What can this mean? Has the house of Ioclus come to grief?" When he arrived, he was told of the fate of Ioclus, and he too mourned. Next arrived Hadrior, only slightly behind Naross, with one thousand warriors of Asylia, each of them sure with the arrow and the javelin. As evening fell Amyntas of Kerion came upon the hill, and with him seven hundred warriors, all of them proven in battle with hardened hands and grim faces, their swords whetted for death. Finally, when tents were pitched, fires struck up and the lords already in counsel, the arrival of Lord Garba of Cadaras was announced, though he only brought with him one hundred men, for he did not want to give the Caeylonics the appearance that he was draining his city.

When all the tents were pitched and the lords had feasted and given orders to their men, they all gathered by a great fire to warm themselves against the frigid autumn winds and hear Manaeth retell the tale of Ioclus' defeat which she had heard from the servant Aön before he perished: how Gygas had went over to Arahaz and led him up to Lissus; how they came upon them quietly, shielded by the storm; how the bold sons of Ioclus fell first, and how Ioclus perished under many blows; how Saraeth her sister was slain, too (and Hadrior wept when he heard this) and how Osseia herself was killed and how Manaeth heard it told from the mouth of the servant, Aön; and how Manaeth herself hurled the spear of Eleth and slew the traitor Gygas upon Lissus, and then of her flight to Cruachan. However, she mentioned nothing about the fountain or the stag.

When Manaeth had retold all of these things, she said to the men gathered, "My lords, I am wasted away with grief and labor. My limbs quake beneath me from want of food, and I can feel the heaviness of sleep descend upon me. Therefore, I will retire to my

44

tent which has been prepared for me, to take my supper and give myself to gentle sleep, the friend of men whose embrace helps to wash sorrow away. I have done my duty, I have acted as a maid of Asylia ought. I have brought forth to you the war spear and mighty shield of Ioclus, my father of happy memory. I have slain the traitor Gygas with my own hand. Therefore, to thyselves I commend the things to now be considered: whether to continue in your plan to prosecute the war or sue for peace, how best to accomplish what is decided upon, and whom is to succeed noble Ioclus as Lord of Asylia. I pray the gods bless you with wisdom! Good night." Then she departed with much weariness to her tent, where three maidens bathed and cleansed her, saw to it that she was fed and warmed and put to sleep on a pile of furs. Thus the five lords of Elabaea were left alone.

Chapter 6
Maid of Asylia

When Manaeth had taken her rest, the five remaining lords of Elabaea gathered around the blazing fire began to debate fiercely amongst themselves. Hadrior spoke first and said, "My lords, this is a great grief, for in a single day I have lost my king, my father-in-law and my wife as well. Though the sorrow is fresh and rending, we cannot put aside our duty. Shall we continue in the plan of Ioclus, or sue for peace? If Ioclus is slain upon Lissus' slopes, then he never made it to Cyrenaica, nor rallied any of the Lugarians or the hill folk to our aid, and we are left alone."

Arrax said, "Damned be the Lugarians and the hill folk! Shall we sue for peace after our king, his sons and daughters are slain in the night? The sword must be met by the sword!" But Naross intervened and said, "My brothers, Manaeth herself tells us of our most pressing need, for before we can decide whether or not to prosecute this war we have embarked upon, we must first select a new lord from among our number to lead Asylia, whether in peace or bloodshed." Then they all fell silent and looked at one another.

It was Amyntas who broke that chill silence first and said, "As the next eldest brother to Ioclus, it seems to me that Naross ought be our rightful lord." Arrax seconded him, but Garba and Hadrior dissented. When they began to argue amongst themselves, Naross silenced them and said, "Were these happier times and had my brother gone down to the grave in peace, I should not object to the words of noble Amyntas. In fact, I should come here boldly and with pride to insist on my rights to my brother's chair. But we are possibly about to embark upon a cruel and bitter war. Were that sturdy Masaros, grim Menelor, or even handsome Eleth here today! Then there would be no question as to who should rule. But I say this: though I may be wise and eldest brother after Ioclus, I am old and advanced in years, as was my brother before me. Were to the gods my sons were still alive! Oh that they had not fallen, slain in battle with the men of Epidymia six years prior. Then if I were to fall the succession would be safe. But alas, I am bereaved of offspring in my old age. Nay, a better choice would be one who is young, deadly with the spear and able to endure the hardships of the campaign. For if Caeylon attacks and I must lead troops into

46

battle and into the wilds, who knows whether I shall be slain by Marudan spear or by the hardships of war, which are beyond my years to bear. Then would we be without direction in the middle of a fierce war, and our resolve would falter. Therefore, let a younger man be chosen."

All present acknowledged Naross' wisdom, so dark-haired Arrax put himself forward and argued passionately for his own position, winning all the lords over except Hadrior. When Arrax perceived that he had not the support of Hadrior, he said angrily, "Why do you hold out when all of your brethren are ready to confirm me? Speak now, thou sly fox, or hold thy tongue forever!" Hadrior said, "Arrax, I doubt not your skill in ruling, nor your deadly aim with the spear. But consider the war we are about to embark upon; Caeylon has never in the time of my father or his father before him been bested in war, leastwise by a small people such as ourselves, fierce though we be! Therefore, if we are to attain victory, our hope lies in the unity of all Elabaeans rather than in the prowess of one."

Then Naross said, "What do you drive at with this, lord Hadrior?" Hadrior replied, "Hear me out my lords, for what I am about to propose fills me with great trembling. What of the maid, Manaeth, daughter of Ioclus? She has by providence been spared the massacre upon Lissus' slopes that took her kin. She is the sole surviving child of Ioclus, to whose house we owe allegiance. As daughter of Ioclus, she is of both the people of Asylia and Cadarasia as well, by virtue of her mother, Grianne, sister to Garba, lord of Cadarasia. Was it not Manaeth herself who slew the traitor Gygas with the spear of her brother? Was it not Manaeth who brought forth the great spear and shield of Ioclus from Lissus to this sacred hill? And was it not Manaeth who came to this place first, and was found here alone by Arrax? Can all these things mean nothing? Nay, it would be too much. I descry in these events the hand of Fate which would have us take Manaeth as our queen."

Arrax frowned and said in great agitation, "Such is not the custom of our people for the daughter of a lord to take his place when he has brothers living still. Such has never been the way of Asylia in former times." But Naross said, "Never have we had times such as this."

Thus they hotly debated the matter into the late hours of the night. Hadrior supported Manaeth for the queenship and won over Amyntas and Naross to his position. Garba, too, declared for

Manaeth, by virtue of her close kinship with him through his sister, Grianne, who had been wife of Ioclus. Arrax alone was slow in accepting her, for he had been near the kingship himself before Hadrior had proposed Manaeth. Shortly before dawn, Arrax consented, having been weighed down by the opinions of the other lords, though from that day forward he bore a seething anger against Hadrior, for he said, "Had he not raised his voice, I should have been made king!"

Thus it was that on the twenty-second day of the tenth month, in the first year of the reign of King Belthazre of Caeylon, at morn upon the rising of the golden sun, the five lords of Elabaea, Naross of Asylia, Arrax of Paros, Amyntas of Kerion, Hadrior, son-in-law of Ioclus and Garba of Cadarasia sent for a herald and said, "Go and fetch the lady Manaeth and bring her hither. Tell her maidens to wash and anoint her and have her made beautiful, and have her bring with her the shield and spear of Ioclus." The herald went unto the tent of Manaeth and told her maidens, "The lords summon Manaeth to their counsel, but first let her be bathed, anointed and made beautiful, for something great is about to happen." The maids did as they were commanded, and waking lady Manaeth they bathed, cleansed and anointed her with oil. Then Manaeth arrayed herself in a splendid gown of green and was wrapped in a white cloak of ermine, and on her head she wore a silver tiara that was delicate and finely wrought. In one hand she clasped the mighty spear of Ioclus her father, and upon her back she slung his great shield of beaten bronze. Then she came forth from her tent, and her train of maidens with her, and walked through the camp to the meeting place of the five lords. And as she walked, the men of Elabaea emerged from their tents as well, and followed behind her, so that all the company of Elabaea was gathered together about her.

When she approached the meeting place of the five lords, she greeted them pleasantly and would have made familiar with them, but they rose and stood before her solemnly, and she perceived that something was amiss and said, "What is this my lords? Is there more grave news?" But Naross spoke boldly and said, "Lady Manaeth, thou blessed among women of Asylia, come and claim the throne of thy father. Take up his scepter and rule this land in might against our cruel foes. Be our queen in peace and war, and we will pledge troth to thee, to fight for thee and serve thee all thy days as our queen and rightful heir to the house of

Ioclus." Then all the men of war gathered around her shouted their assent and clashed their spears and shields.

When Manaeth understood that they purposed to make her queen, her knees trembled and she pleaded with the lords with great cries, begging that she was not worthy for such an undertaking, that as recently as two days ago she had been lost hopelessly in the wilderness, that she had left her family alone and been allowed to live while they suffered death. With many such sayings and a great many tears she protested, but Naross said, "Lady Manaeth, these things were all by providence, that you should be given to us as our ruler in this dire hour. Resign yourself to your fate." When Naross had said this, Manaeth ceased her weeping and assented to all that they proposed and consented to be made Queen of Asylia.

Then horns were blown and all of the men of war assembled on the hill, near where Manaeth and the lords stood. Then seven of the stongest men were brought forth, and they bore Manaeth aloft, sitting her upon the shield of Ioclus her father. Naross took the spear of Ioclus in hand, and began a procession from that spot up to the Stone of Cruachan, which crested the hill about five hundred paces from where they stood. Behind Naross processed Arrax, then Hadrior, then Garba and lastly Amyntas, who walked before Manaeth. Then was carried Manaeth, daughter of Ioclus and heir to the rulership of Asylia. Before her came maidens of great beauty who danced and sung sweet melodies of Asylia in the spring, and behind her marched a solemn column of a thousand warriors, all battle hardened and keen with spear and sword. As they approached the hill, the men began to chant one of the solemn hymns of Asylia, ancient and sonorous, praising the virtues of just lordship and invoking the blessing of heaven upon the young queen, recalling to mind the divine parentage of the house of Ioclus.

When the procession reached the Stone of Cruachan, Manaeth removed her shoes and stepped forth from the shield, standing aloft upon the stone, so that she was above all the other lords and men upon the hill top. Then Naross came forth and recited in verse all of the great deeds of the house of Manaeth, from the very beginning unto that day, and all the assembly stood silent with great reverence. And what did Naross sing of that autumn morn? First he sung of the wanderings of Laban in the ancient days, he who came forth out of the east with his kin and established a kingdom in the west, in Elabaea, which is named from Laban. The whole genealogy was recited, how Laban begat four sons who scattered and settled the west, and how it was his grandson, Anrothan, who wed the beautiful maiden Cyréa, and brought forth the Asylian people. He sung of Eamon, son of Anrothan, who begot the lovely and renowned Orianna by Evarista, and how Orianna was secluded away because of her great beauty until the day when she was spotted by Manx in the far north and carried off to Eriar, bride to a god. He sung of the love of Manx and Orianna, and then of the birth of Orix, that most glorious of all warriors. He told of how Orix followed a wild horse to the foothills of the highlands of Cyria, and in their shadow founded the city of Asylia and built with his own hands the mighty Hall of Orix, from whence every lord of Asylia reigned thereafter. Then he sung of Ancyrus, grandson of Orix, who was a mighty warlord in his day and won the hand of fellowship of none other than King Dyans of Epidymia, first ruler of that land and excelled by none save Anathar in wisdom, splendor and power. Finally the song came down to Manaeth's own day, and of the glories of Ioclus her father in war and peace, how he had slain many Epidymians and killed the great boar of Gihon. When Naross reached the end of his song, he added a new verse, praising the valor of Manaeth and her slaying of the traitor Gygas atop the slopes of Lissus. When the song had ended, everybody stood silent.

Then Manaeth was handed the spear of Ioclus and the mighty shield which she had been born upon, and she took these up in her hands and held them aloft to the winds, invoking their aid in battle. After this she said, "Men of Asylia, never has it been known in the days of our fathers unto our most distant ancestors that a queen has ruled the people of our land. What the lords have done this day in proclaiming me is something new in Asylia, but something that will confound our enemies and bring crashing victory to our cause, though it come at the cost of much spilt blood." Then she decreed that henceforth she should no longer be known as Manaeth, but by the name Manissa, which means "Maid of Asylia." Then all of the men there assembled clashed their spears to their shields and cried out as one, "Hail Manissa, Queen of Asylia! We will serve thee forever!" As they cried, Manissa stood tall upon the stone and seemed to grow in stature and grandeur, so that even Arrax was fearful of her might. And the sun fell and lighted upon her, so that she seemed at that moment to become exceedingly beautiful and glorious, like one of the Mighty Ones of old. And many of the men there bowed their faces to the ground and said, "The beauty of Orianna and Osseia lives in Manissa, and the might of Manx and Orix her forebears!" Never had Manissa appeared so fearsome or beautiful as that day she stood upon the Stone of Cruachan when the Asylians proclaimed her queen.

After all this, Manissa came down from the stone and the whole assembly, lords and common soldiers, had a great feast in honor of the young queen. Then as night fell, Manissa retired to her tent to speak of stratagems with the five lords. And on that night it was decided by them to continue in the plans of Ioclus and make savage war upon Maruda, to utterly drive the men of Caeylon from the land and destroy the oppressive stronghold of Danath Hered. When they had resolved upon this course they drank and made many oaths of loyalty and then retired late after darkness fell. And the shrill winds of autumn night were upon the land.

Manissa was greatly emboldened and a spirit of fire burned within her, and she said, "Never again will the men of Maruda take us unaware by night. We shall strike them with great wrath." Then the Asylians struck camp and left Cruachan, taking to the wilderness, as had been the plan of Ioclus. All remained in the company of Manissa, save Garba, who returned to Cadaras. They traversed the lands of the west, proclaiming a new Queen of Asylia and everywhere swelling their ranks with hardy Asylian men weary of Caeylonic rule. They also drew to them hillmen of Bados, many Cadarasians, some fighters of Lugar and mercenaries of Ituria, and not a few men of Epidymia. When the nights grew long and snows began to fall, Manissa came forth from the wilderness into the region around Cadarasia and struck a Caeylonic caravan with the sword, slaying two hundred men of Caeylon and taking much plunder. Thus she did for the remainder of the winter, and before long word was spread among the Marudans of a fierce warrior maiden who rode with the Asylians and gave speed and strength to their arms. The men of Caeylon grew greatly afraid, so that no caravans of merchants or units of soldiers would venture too far from Danath Hered.

But every place Manissa went, people came out to greet her and men were eager to join her throng. By midwinter's eve the warriors following Manissa had swelled to some five thousand, and many more had pledged their service in the spring, when the thaws would come. Therefore Arrax came to her and said, "These several months we have been victorious in waging war against Caeylon by ambush and stealth and have been highly favored, but our numbers have become too great to continue such. I counsel thee, my queen and my beloved niece, that we should divide our warriors up into companies of hundreds and of thousands, and set some lord or battle-proven warrior over each thousand. Then we must meet the men of Caeylon in open war. Only when we defeat them in open war will Belthazre relent in his purposes." This advice seemed good to Manissa, and so she divided her army into five companies of one thousand each: one led by Amyntas, one by Naross, one by Hadrior, one under Arrax and one under Manissa. The one thousand who served under Manissa called themselves "The Sword of Our Lady." Having arranged her army and put it in order, Manissa thus brought them to a halt on the broad plains of An Erras west of the Brook of Erriad, near the borders of Asylia going eastward towards Cadarasia. There they camped for the duration of the winter and laid plans for the ruin of Maruda.

Word of Manissa, her raids and her growing army spread east, and when it reached Belthazre from the west that an heiress of Ioclus was alive and was making open war upon the Marudans, he seethed with rage. Narússa came in before him and said, "Did I not tell you? You have hesitated these many months, and the countryside is in revolt against your lordship. Therefore, issue your mighty command; proclaim a decree sealed with your royal signal that the men of Caeylon are to make war on the Asylians and all who aid them." Belthazre assented and sent three-thousand hardened Kushite warriors into the west to reinforce Arahaz at Danath Hered. With them he sent an order to Arahaz, saying, "Burn the villages of the Asylians. Slay all the males, but bring the women as slaves back to Maruda. If any village surrenders and pledges fealty to the King of Caeylon, you shall spare their lives, but burn their homes nonetheless and send the people eastward into captivity, that they might labor in the mines here in Caeylon. And slay for me the woman pretender who claims to be the heir of Ioclus. If any man of Caeylon will not fight or is afraid to venture forth into the wilds, slay him and have his body trampled beneath the feet of the army as they go out of the gates in the morning, as is the custom in Caeylon." Thus the men of Caeylon were sorely troubled, being afraid to go out because of Manissa but afraid of the penalties Belthazre commanded to Arahaz on those who held back.

Then Arahaz called one of his captains, a Baazite from the Southlands named Tegleth, and said, "Our lord is wrathful over the incursions of the Asylians against our men and shall hold us responsible if the pretender Manissa is not brought to heel. Our spies tell us she is encamped somewhere in the region of An Erras, west of the Erriad. Therefore, as soon as the snows begin to melt and the spring is upon us, go out into the wilderness and destroy the rebels. Take with you the three-thousand Kushites recently sent to us by our king, in addition to two-thousand footsoldiers from Danath Hered and five hundred charioteers." Tegleth said, "It shall be done my lord." This Tegleth was an exceedingly fearsome foe, for he was accounted the largest of all the men of Baaz and stood a cubit and a half above all others. His skin was dark and rough from years of campaigning in the hot sands of the east and the cruel regions of the Southlands, and he wore about him the skin of a great lion which he had slain in Capaldia. He bore a gleaming battlesword of whetted bronze, longer than the height of many men, and donned in war a glorious brazen helm, gilded in gold, atop which fluttered a great plume of dark horsehair from a thick crest. His power was immense and he relished feats of strength, and it is said that in Caeylon he had hurled a boulder thirty paces which no other man could even lift. When he cried out in battle, the bones of his foes quaked with fear, and many said he was descended from some ogre or giant, or that he was one of the Mighty Ones of old. As winter wore on and the snows persisted, Tegleth brooded about the halls of Danath Hered, considering how best to meet Manissa in battle. And he made a vow at the altar of Nergal in Danath Hered to tear the living heart of Manissa from her breast and eat it on the field of battle. He was thus consumed with bloodlust, and eagerly anticipated the lengthening of the days, that he should ride forth from Danath Hered to slaughter and destruction.

By and by the snows began to recede, flowers and grasses began to come forth from beneath their white beds, and the warmth of the sun returned to the land. On the very day that the snows receded from the valley betwixt Cadaras and Danath Hered and it was told that the roads were clear, Tegleth gave the command for the army to muster on the plain and be ready to depart three days hence. Then word was brought to Manissa at An Erras-by-Erriad, saying, "The Caeylonics have mustered several thousand men on the plains outside Cadaras and are marching forthwith into this region, and the foul Baazite commanding them has vowed to eat thy heart!" Then Arrax leapt up, filled with hot anger, and said, "By the beard of Manx, that desert dog will regret those words! I will feed him indeed, but with dirt from the earth when I bring his mighty frame down in death!" But Manissa calmed him, and gave word to her captains that the army be drawn up upon the plains and made ready to march by nightfall.

Chapter 7
Arrax Unleashed

Tegleth the Baazite, a man of great prowess and might, led the army of Maruda out of Danath Hered and the region of Cadarasia on the fifth day of the third month under the bright sun of the Elabaean spring. With him were three-thousand Kushite spearmen from his own country, two thousand men of war from Danath Hered who had served many years in the west, and five hundred charioteers in full Marudan battle dress wielding deadly spears. Each chariot was driven by a skilled driver who bore a bow and was able to fire while directing the car. Tegleth himself rode a great chariot of bronze pulled by a team of four black chargers and raised his spear aloft as he led the army forth. Lord Garba watched him depart from Cadaras, and as soon as the legions of men had disappeared down the road in dust and cloud, he called for his fastest runners and sent them west through the wilderness to warn Manissa and the Asylians about the coming of Tegleth and to give her word concerning their numbers.

Manissa's army had already broke camp and was moving eastward across the plain when the runner from Garba reached her and told her of the army of Tegleth and its strength. Then Naross said, "My lady, at best they cannot be but two days march east of here. Shall we cross the Erriad and meet them on the eastern shores?" But Manissa said, "No. Let us rather make haste to the brook and destroy the fords there to slow their progress. We will then withdraw and allow them to cross the river, but when they have crossed it so that their advance parties are upon the plain but their rearguard still in the water, we shall strike them, with their backs to the stream. Thus we shall throw them into utter confusion and render their chariots useless." This seemed good to the other lords, and so a hundred picked men under Amyntas made haste and rode through the night to the Fords of Erriad. They worked until sunup digging away the ford so that in its place they left many deep trenches in the water. They returned to Manissa the following day, who by then was but a half-day journey from the brook. She said to her lords, "We will march on till nightfall and arrange our forces just out of bowshot from the waters." When they arrived at dusk they found the fords destroyed, as Amyntas had

55

reported, and the Marudans nowhere to be seen. Thus they encamped upon the far slide of a gently sloping hillock on the western shore of the brook and made plans for the coming fray.

It was late into the night when the drums of Caeylon were first heard ringing in the hillsides near the Brook of Erriad, and it is told that the sun rose pink on the frosty morn upon the plains when Tegleth called his army to a halt east of the crystal waters of Erriad. As day dawned and the mists cleared, he beheld clearly the forces of Manissa encamped upon the far reaches of the brook and drawn up in battle lines, ready for war. Two thousand cavalry made up her front line, behind which stood three thousand more warriors on foot, each armed with spear and shield of Asylian fashion. Before them all he saw Manissa herself, seated upon Ruah and brandishing the spear of Ioclus, its head shimmering in the morning sun. When Tegleth beheld them, the wrath of his vow returned to him and he was enflamed with bloodlust. Thus he commanded his men to advance, and the ranks of Caeylon began their crossing of the Erriad. Several of the Kushite spearmen advanced first, followed by the charioteers. Though the waters were not deep, the destruction the the fords caused many of the chariot wheels to become mired in the sand and the ranks of Tegleth became confused as some crossed over, some remained on the far side, and some got bogged down in the water. Tegleth raged and whipped the chariot drivers with a lash of cords, but they remained mired in the stream, and as more men passed through, the riverbed turned ever more to mud.

It was thus when one third only of Tegleth's men had crossed over Erriad and were still forming up on the opposite shore that Manissa crashed the mighty spear of Ioclus against her shield and cried "Cruacha!" Then all the men of Asylia roared "Cruacha!" and swept down upon the Marudans with great fury. The Kushite spearmen braced themselves and trained their spears on the riders, bringing some down with skillful throws, but the horsemen of Asylia were undaunted and came crashing into the dark men of the east, trampling them underfoot and scattering them utterly. Amyntas led the charge, his long hair whipping about him as he turned his horse this way and that, now hurling a spear into the back of some fleeing Marudan, now striking with his sword and gashing the throat of some swarthy desert fighter foolhardy enough to charge his horse. The Kushite lines wavered, then broke and turned, heading back to the stream. Amyntas led his riders along the edge of the water, harassing those attempting the crossing with spear and arrow. One certain captain of Caeylon, Ungorah of Lyson, rallied his men and led them across the stream amidst the fierce attacks of Amyntas. There he gained a foothold on the other side of the waters and gave succor to the men attempting to cross there, so that many scores began coming over to the Asylian side. Then Amyntas said, "By the gods, I will bring this fellow down who thinks to make a safe crossing here!" Then he took aim and cast his spear at Ungorah, and it caught him soundly in the stomach as he was raising his sword to lead more men up the banks. He toppled to the ground in agony and pulled the spear from his belly, and with it his guts came spilling out. Thus perished Ungorah, and Amyntas shoved his corpse down the bank and into the cold waters of the Erriad. When the Marudans saw it floating they trembled and began to flee back away from the banks and the arm of Amyntas. And as many who were caught in the gleam of his eye were brought low by his deadly aim. Thus Amyntas won glory that day.

But Hadrior was driven back, as Tegleth had reformed some of his Kushite spearmen on the right and brought over some of the Marudan infantry as well. They had made a mighty cast of spears against Hadrior which slew many of his advance guard and put them to rout. But Naross saw this and ordered his men forward, and there was fierce hand to hand combat all along the southwestern bank of the brook, near the grove of poplars that still stands there to this day. Though the Caeylonic men pressed hard and dropped many brave Asylians with their arrows and spears, the company of Naross and Hadrior held fast, but neither could they drive the Caeylonics back into the river.

Then Manissa mounted Ruah her steed and cried out to her company, "Remember Osseia!" They rode forward with great fury and hurled themselves into the charioteers and small companies of soldiers who were attempting a foothold on the western side of the bank. The men of Manissa fought gallantly from horseback, striking at the Marudans whenever they dared expose face or breast to their flesh-biting spearheads. But soon the ground beneath them was turned to a choking mire, and the horses of the Asylians became bogged down alongside the chariots of the Marudans, and westerner and easterner fought hand to hand in the mud, grappling and choking in deathly combat, blood and gore mingling with dirt and grime in the hideous battlefield. Manissa dismounted Ruah and spied Tegleth raging about on the western bank, wielding his great sword with much rage and cleaving Asylians in two, so that even the company of Amyntas fled before him. Then she aimed the spear of Ioclus and hurled it with great strength at Tegleth, but it missed its mark and instead hit his chariot driver, striking him in the side and sending him crying into the dirt. But this enraged Tegleth, as it caused him to come down from his car. When he entered the melee on foot he was the tallest man on the battlefield, and he cried out with a roar like a lion in anger, swinging his sword wildly against the Asylians, hewing off the arms and heads of man and horse alike and bearing death about him wherever he roamed.

But as Naross and Hadrior fought, they were slowly pushed back into the trees, and the way was opened for many of the Caeylonics massing on the opposite bank of the river to cross over. These men lunged across the Erriad in scores, and soon reinforced their companions in assaulting the position of Naross and Hadrior, who became entrapped in the poplars on the southwest ridge of the river. They fought valiantly, but soon all of their spears and arrows were expended and there remained to them only their swords. The Marudans moved up and surrounded the hillock upon which the trees stood and would have charged them right there, but an officer in charge of the Marudans stepped forward and called, "Why throw your lives away needlessly? Let your lords identify themselves and send delegates to come discuss terms with us." Naross, who was crouched in the tall grass behind some of the trees beside Hadrior, called out, "We are Naross and Hadrior, lords of Asylia both and kinsmen of Ioclus, in former days our king, who was slain treacherously by your nation in the night, and we have no words to exchange with you. Therefore, gird up your loins like a man and take this hill if you can! We may perish, but not before we send many a man among you to the shades."

When the officer heard this, he removed his helm and laughed, saying, "Fate is strange indeed! For I heard you say you were the lords Naross and Hadrior! We have met before, my lords, for when Arahaz first came from Danath Hered seeking Osseia, I was with him in the delegation sent to the Hall of Orix to fetch her. And you played deceptively with us, and told us they were simply out hunting! Liars, all of you! I begged my master that we should slay you at once, for I perceived your treachery. But he would have none of it. But I got my vengeance for my wasted time, for I was again sent with Arahaz when he tracked Ioclus' house in the wilderness with the aid of Gygas the betrayer, and I was among those men who cast their spears into the sons of thy late king and slew them. And now I shall have the glory of extinguishing his house here this day!"

Naross, when he heard this, was greatly enraged and shook with anger. Then he said to Hadrior, "Shall we suffer this insolent braggart to go unpunished, who boasts of slaying our kin, and your wife and my brother among them?" Then gray-headed Naross searched about in the grasses and found a small stone, about the size of a man's fist. As the officer finished his boast, Naross emerged from behind the trees and cast the stone with a great strength beyond his years. The rock struck the officer between the nose and forehead and sent him crashing to the ground with much blood. His eyes rolled into his head and he answered no one who called to him, and thus he perished. When the Marudans saw that he had been killed by the stone hurled by old Naross, they were thrown into fear, and Naross perceived their terror. Then Naross called a charge, and his men and those of Hadrior rushed from the tree grove and flooded down the hill with cries of "Cruacha!" in their mouths and flame in their eyes. They cut down many of the Marudans, and many more turned to flee back across the Brook of Erriad, but Naross and Hadrior pursued them with a great slaughter. It is told in other tales how after the battle was over, Hadrior cut out the tongue of the bragging Caeylonic officer and nailed it as a memorial to the tree from which Naross threw the stone. And ever after Naross was known as "Naross of the Great Throw" till the end of his days.

It was sometime before this that bold Arrax led his men, infantry all, into the fray and saw that Manissa's company was bogged down in the mud of the stream, that the men of Amyntas were fleeing in rout before Tegleth, and that Naross and Hadrior were sorely pressed in the poplar wood at the far end of the battlefield. Furthermore, he espied several more companies of Caeylonic troops still massed on the far side of the river waiting to come across when the lines should clear. Then his blood boiled hot and he cried to his men, "Prove thyselves now true sons of thy country and water our sacred ground in the blood of these foreigners!" He formed his men up in two long lines, each man's shield covering the flank of the man beside him, cruel spears lowered thirsty for death. On the flanks of these lines he set his infantry. Then he donned his war helm and took up the lead on foot, pressing towards the hottest area of the battle, where Tegleth was cutting a swath of death about him with his gore-soaked blade. The men of Arrax thundered into the melee, bringing doom to all who withstood them.

Then a great fury possessed Arrax, and a rage unchecked, and he gathered to himself several spears in his left hand and with his right made deadly casts. With one throw he brought down Anrath, an experienced captain of Maruda who had spent ten years in Elabaea. Then he cast again and slew Gorah, a kinsman of Arahaz who had been present on Lissus when Ioclus and Osseia were slain. This Gorah approached Arrax and threw his spear at him, but the head crumpled against Arrax's armor. He turned to flee, but Arrax hurled his spear and pierced him through the back, leaving him groping in the mud. With two more throws Arrax brought down two Kushite war chiefs who had fought in many battles in the east, but they would return there no more, for their corpses fell on the muddy banks of Erriad. When he perceived the Marudan captain Ormuz attempting to rally those fleeing from the sortie of Naross, he took aim and made his cast, striking Ormuz under the right breast and toppling him from his chariot. When he fell, his legs became entangled in the harness, and his horses fled driverless, dragging their master limp through the dirt behnd them. Everywhere Arrax went he cast his deadly spears and struck men down into the mire.

It was then that he espied Manissa sorely pressed in the muddiest region of the battlefield, entangled in a mass of Marudans and Asylians making fierce war with each other in the mire. She was covered in gore and dirt and struck blows this way and that with the spear of her father, which she had recovered; yet nevertheless her enemies were closing about her and her own warriors fell quickly. Then black-haired Arrax unsheathed his flesh ripping sword and thew himself into the combat like a mad dog. His blade slashed this way and that, a beam of light in the cold morning sun. Everywhere he went men fell before him, and no one could stand up to his might. Swords and spears raised against him were broken, shields cloven in two, and armor was as linen before his biting blade. He roared and battled and slew scores of men who stood before him. Then the Marudans said, "The gods possess that man! We must flee or perish!" Many of them fled across the stream to escape the fury of Arrax, whose mind was bent on doom. Then

Manissa was relieved, and rested for a time.

But cruel Arrax did not halt his rage and instead plunged into the brook, bringing the battle to the Marudan side of the stream. His men followed behind, clashing spear upon shield and breaking the power of Caeylon in every engagement, leaving corpses in their path. The battle became a rout, and the Caeylonics dropped their spears and shields and ran from the battle with terrible swiftness. If there was any man who looked back, or stopped to pant, or halted to fetch some item, or retrieve a fallen comrade, or slowed for any other reason, that same man was caught in the furious path of Arrax and brought down to death. When Tegleth saw that the battle had become a rout, that Naross and Hadrior had fought their way from the trees and that Arrax was pressing the battle to the Marudan side of the river, he roared like a wounded bear and took off after Arrax in pursuit. The men of Amyntas and some of Hadrior's warriors pursued him, but Tegleth picked up the axle rod of a broken chariot and swung it about him with great wrath, and as many Asylians who came within the reach of his swing had their brains dashed or their bones broken. Thus Tegleth raged throughout the Asylian ranks in pursuit of Arrax and crossed over the river.

Then some of Arrax's men called him from his slaughter and said, "Look, lord! The Baazite giant comes seeking your head!" Hot-blooded Arrax turned and said, "It is not I but he who shall go down to death this day!" He selected the sturdiest of all his spears, took hold of his shield firmly and planted his feet on the earth awaiting the approach of Tegleth. When the men saw this, they backed away from him, fearful of the approach of the Baazite, and left Arrax alone. When Tegleth approached, he dropped the axle rod and unsheathed his sword, which was longer in length than Arrax stood tall. Then he called out, "Come, Arrax son of Ancyrus, and I will cake this blade in thy blood! I will feast on the heart of your Asylian wench before the setting of the sun this day." Then he whirled his great blade about and brought it crashing upon the shield of Arrax with a force that made the very bones of the Asylian lord quake and his teeth ring. He pounded at Arrax time and again, each time bringing all his might to bear and hoping to cleave him in two, but sure-footed Arrax held his ground and buffered the heavy blows with his shield, though he could not make a shot with his spear because of the fury of Tegleth's assault. Then Tegleth roared like a fiend of the underworld and brought his sword down with great rage, cleaving the shield of Arrax in two. Massive Tegleth laughed and scorned Arrax, insulting both the house of Ioclus and Manissa and promised again to feast on her flesh as he swept his blade at the Asylian, but to no avail as Arrax was quick footed.

Then Arrax said, "I must take my shot soon or this fight will wear me down." He waited until Tegleth brought his blade down again, and when the giant did so he dodged to the left, but thrust his spear into the side of the giant so that the blade went in under his armpit. Tegleth howled in agony and was no longer able to hold his sword, and it fell uselessly to the earth. Then Arrax pulled his spear forth and cried out, "Death now comes to you at my hands beast of Belthazre!" Then he struck again and pushed the brazen spearhead into the throat of Tegleth above the collarbone, flesh-rending metal piercing skin and bone. Blood poured forth from the wound of Tegleth like a waterfall, and the Baazite giant gurgled and collapsed to his knees. Then Arrax drew his sword from the scabbard and plunged it into the bowels of Tegleth, doubling him over and bringing him crashing to the dirt. When the men of Caeylon saw Tegleth fall, they turned on their heels and fled. Then Manissa called a pursuit and the Marudans were harried all that day with a great slaughter, nor did the Asylians turn back until the setting of the sun. Afterward Amyntas returned and said, "My lady, we have pursued the Marudans with a great slaughter and have felled many bodies in the wilderness. Few indeed shall return to Danath Hered!" Manissa said, "Perhaps it is better that some should return to Arahaz to tell of the great deeds done here today."

But Arrax, as he had vowed, severed the head of Tegleth and stuffed it full of mud, saying, "You who vowed before thy cruel gods to feast on the heart of Manissa, did I not swear that I would both kill thee and stuff thy mouth with dirt for its vile curses?" Then he came before Manissa and hurled the head of Tegleth at her feet, saying, "Thus have I defended thy honor, my queen." And all the camp of the Asylians cheered. But Manissa looked to the setting sun, pondered and said, "Were I any other maiden, and my father Ioclus still ruling over fair Asylia, and were our land at peace, then would I be dressed in silks and finery, my hair done up in tresses, and would noble lords court me with gentle gifts and sweet promises of love. But instead I am covered in gore and filth, and the only dowry I receive is the bloody head of this ignoble braggart." Then she kicked the head of Tegleth and sent it rolling into the Erriad. It was said in later days that the head of Tegleth washed up far off in the land of Lugaria and a tree with black bark grew where it landed, for so is it told among the Lugarians to this day.

But as for the great sword of Tegleth, Arrax took it as an heirloom of his house and affixed it in his hall above the fragments of his broken shield, which Tegleth had cloven in his fury.

Chapter 8
Of Cadarasia and Danath Hered

The slaying of Tegleth and routing of the Caeylonics did not bring peace but only war to Asylia and more grief to Manissa. Lord Garba of Cadarasia watched anxiously for any word of the battle, and when he saw the remnants of the Caeylonic force straggling back to Danath Hered, weary and forlorn, he understood that there had been a great victory for Manissa. Then he gathered together the chiefs of the great houses of the city of Cadarasia and said to them, "To arms! Manissa has defeated Tegleth the Baazite and will be coming east soon. Therefore, let every man be ready to take up arms and make war on the Marudans when the time is right, only take care not to give any sign of what we are planning to do, lest the Marudans fall upon us prematurely." But the spies of Arahaz were everywhere, and when Tegleth had marched out, Arahaz took note of runners leaving and returning to Cadaras. Then his spies returned to him and said, "Something is amiss in Cadaras, for all of the people are in great anxiety and Garba keeps his counsels to himself." Arahaz said, "It is plain what is occuring: Garba is in league with Manissa and plans to make war on us as soon as he is reinforced from the west! The fall of Tegleth has made these Elabaeans haughty and arrogant. We must chastize them!"

So Arahaz called forth the entire garrison of Danath Hered and formed them up on the plains outside Cadaras, some three thousand men in all. He also sent for men to come from the surrounding fortresses which ringed in the land of Elabaea, and out of the six other strongholds came nigh unto three thousand men. He also gathered Badoan and Illyr mercenaries from the south, one thousand in number, and a contingent of cavalry sent from Caina in Caeylon, which is only six days from Cadaras, numbering six hundred. Thus the total amount of his forces which he massed on the plains of Cadaras was near seven thousand six hundred. Then Garba sent emissaries to him asking why the Marudans were threatening Cadaras with their forces and whether or not Arahaz would be willing to meet with Garba in council to redress their grievances. Garba did this to stall Arahaz from any action until Manissa should come into the region with the other lords of Elabaea. But Arahaz responded, "I know what you are up to, Garba son of Gorba! With one hand you pledge peace and friendship to

64

the men of Caeylon, and with the other you aid that Asylian witch against me! I know that you were at the council in the Hall of Orix when Ioclus first raised the spear of rebellion, for so it was told to me by Gygas when he betrayed Ioclus to me. I know also that you have pledged fealty to this Manissa, daughter of Ioclus, as your rightful master and that you wish ill upon our troops when we go out for battle. I know as well (for my spies have told me) that you are sending your women and children into hiding and arming your men, hoping to make war upon Danath Hered and drive us from the land. This you hope to do with Manissa, whom you await from the west. But it shall not be so! Gird yourself and defend your city the best you know how, for this day the wrath of Caeylon falls on you all, and you shall see how Belthazre rewards traitors!" Arahaz gave this message to the emissary and said also to him, "Come forth with no more messages from Garba. The day you do you shall surely die." Then he sent him away.

When Garba heard the response of Arahaz, he told his captains, "Make ready for war!" Thus it was that seven days after the defeat of Tegleth at Erriad, the armies of Caeylon mustered on the plains outside Cadaras, and Arahaz gave the command to advance upon the city. They advanced from the plain and surrounded the city, then set fire to all the fields and slew any Cadarasians caught outside the walls. Then Arahaz said, "Go up and take the city! Strike it with the sword!" The Caeylonics advanced rank on rank, trampelling the grass into mud beneath them. Garba and his people made a valiant defense of the city, for if anywhere the Caeylonics started to break through, Garba appeared with his spear to thrust them out. If one captain fell defending a section of the wall, Garba ran up to take his place and drive the Marudans back. But the walls of Cadaras were weak, for when the Marudans first came into the land they carted off all the stone in the region to Caeylon and later forbid the Cadarasians from reinforcing their walls in any way. Thus it took but a single afternoon for the men of Caeylon to breach the walls in several places, so that Garba and his warriors had to withdraw to the citadel at the center of the city. The ranks of Maruda advanced through the outer city, torching all the buildings and slaughtering any who were caught within their reach, man and woman alike. But Garba fortified the citadel, the old Temple of Mironna, and with the greater part of his warriors made a stand from there. The place was assailed all through the evening and held fast, for it was built of stone and of a very great height. Nevertheless, close to day break, the Marudans gained a foothold on the western side of the citadel and could not be dislodged. A troupe of Marudan soldiers leapt down in the midst of the temple precinct and, fighting furiously, made their way to the gates and flung them open to the Caeylonics outside. The Caeylonics rushed into the temple with their spears thirsty for blood, trampelling and spearing those in their path. Garba roused his warriors and made a last stand in the courtyard of the temple, and through the fury of his sword arm and the cries of his voice almost succeeded in pushing the Marudans back. But Arahaz ordered his men to scale the walls of the citadel and take the high places, and arrows and javelins rained down upon Garba from above, behind and before him. When he perceived that all was lost, he raised his sword and charged the Caeylonic ranks with a roar in his mouth and was run through with several spears upon the pavement of the courtyard. His voice faltered, his sword dropped to the ground and his blood spilled out, staining the stonework of the sacred precinct. Thus perished Garba, lord of Cadaras, brother-in-law and comrade in arms to noble Ioclus.

When Arahaz saw that Garba was slain, he gave a great shout, and the men of Caeylon advanced rank on rank and overcame the last resistance in the citadel. The Cadarasians, seeing themselves pinned down on all sides with no hope of escape, sought death by their own hands and fell on their swords, thus depriving the Marudans of the slaughter they had been anticipating. When Arahaz had the citadel cleansed, his men removed three thousand bodies and burned them in the valley between Cadaras and Danath Hered. Then the statue of Mironna in the temple was pulled down and smashed, and an idol to Mardu was set up in its place. The walls of Cadaras were entirely demolished and many of the houses burned; only the walls of the citadel were left intact. Then Arahaz said, "This taking and burning of Cadarasia, that den of sedition, has been long overdue. But it was a mere trifle, an exercise for an afternoon. The true battle awaits, when we shall confront that pretender who calls herself Manissa and yet send her to Caeylon in chains." Then Arahaz sent a detachment of his troops up the valley under Irdivan to guard the roads to Cadarasia from the west while the rest of his forces retired to Danath Hered.

But spring was upon the wildlands as Manissa moved her

Asylians on the new moon of the fourth month away from the regions around the Erriad into the southeast, going towards Cadarasia, albeit in a round about way. She had meant to depart sooner but was unable to do so, for all of the surrounding clans and even distant nations as far as Cyrenaica had heard of the victory over Tegleth and sent emissaries to do homage to Manissa, and the ranks of her army swelled, so that her captains had to appoint other captains under them for the management of the scores of men who were daily flocking to her camp in the wilderness. It was nigh on a fortnight after the fall of Cadaras that word finally came to Manissa that the City on the Plain had been overthrown and Garba slain, along with many of his men. When Manissa heard this she wept bitterly, for Garba had been brother to Grianne, mother of Manissa. Then Manissa summoned her lords before her and said, "By the beard of Manx this Arahaz will pay for his treachery! Never was it known in our land from the days of our remotest ancestors that a people as peaceful as the Cadarasians or a lord as noble as Garba were slain on so little a pretext. We shall go forthwith to Danath Hered, and when we see it we shall level it to the ground and take this Arahaz back to Asylia to do judgment upon him."

Hadrior said, "My lady, supposing we get to Danath Hered, it is a very great fortress of the kind found in Caeylon and is mightier than anything built by Asylians and Cadarasians, for we love the wilderness and the plains and loathe being cluttered up in dank fortresses. But with the men of Caeylon it is different: they will shut themselves up inside their fortress and deny us battle. How shall we overthrow this place?"

Manissa said, "Brother-in-law, what you say has some truth in it. But let us first fight our way to Danath Hered and encompass it about, then once our enemies are pinned within we shall set our minds to work on how to destroy them."

Then she gave the battle call, and the hosts encamped upon the plain formed ranks. Manissa sent Amyntas and Arrax among the troops to number them, and at the end of the day they reported ten thousand men who wielded the sword among their army, three thousand of them on horseback. Then Manissa donned her green cloak, took up the great spear of Ioclus and called the march, and the hosts of Asylia and Elabaea moved eastward across the plains. All of the first day they crossed the bleak plains of the Díndumon until they came into the marshy regions of Avlos and Elos and their surrounding villages, all of which had been deserted when the smoke of Cadaras was seen on the horizon. It took Manissa some time to traverse these wetlands, and the infantrymen suffered worst, not only because of the wetness and discomfort, but because the marshlands were inhabited by a certain poisonous breed of snake called the blue adder that struck several of the men and caused them to die. After two days the Asylians had passed southward into drier land and the region of Molossía just southwest of Cadarasia. The land of Molossía is very rocky and spotted with many hillocks and caverns, within which the Asylians pitched camp at the end of the third day. On the fourth day they broke camp early and made their way ten leagues through the wilderness of Molossía until coming upon the borders of Cadarasia shortly before dusk. When she reached Cadarasia, Manissa sent forth two scouts, brothers from Kerion, Rammeth and Eridax by name, and told them to ride into Cadarasia and see if they could spy any movement of the Caeylonics or get any sure estimate of their forces.

Thus Rammeth and Eridax rode forth from the northern marches of Molossía in the evening and by nightfall came upon an outpost of Marudans encamped on the road near the convergence of two forests about two leagues north of the Asylian camp. Young and eager for glory, the brothers decided to attack, for they perceived the outpost to be manned by three men only. Thus they charged the outpost and threw their spears, each hitting their mark and bringing down two men of Caeylon. But the third man raised a cry, and several more Marudans came forth from the woods. Then Rammeth and Eridax saw their folly, for the other soldiers of the outpost had been in the trees gathering firewood and their true strength was greater than the brothers had supposed. Thus they turned their horses to flee, but the Marudans drew bows and fired several arrows at them, and one struck Rammeth in the back between the shoulder blades and knocked him from his horse. Eridax went back to recover him, but the Caeylonics fired heavily upon him and forced him to withdraw. Then Rammeth was captured alive, and after his wound was treated, they put him to torment and found that he had been with Manissa. Then they sent him to Danath Hered with utmost haste, which was but a night's ride eastward.

When Eridax returned to the camp and reported what had happened, Arrax was wroth with him and said, "You come back telling us nothing about the enemy's strength, but have in course

68

lost your brother alive, who will no doubt be put to the torture and reveal everything. As surely as I live you ought to be put to death for this!" But Manissa soothed the rage of her uncle and said, "Eridax has committed a grave fault, for he ought to have listened in stealth to the speech of the men rather than attack them. But it cannot now be undone. We must break camp immediately and march to Danath Hered this very night before the Marudans have a chance to mount their defences. Then the Asylians were roused (for it was close to midnight) and Manissa called the march in the early hours of the morning. When they came to the place Eridax had described, they found the Caeylonic outpost abandoned, for they had known the Asylians were in the region and had withdrawn. Thus Manissa marched throughout the night through the light forests of southwestern Cadarasia until she came near the plains of Cadaras and the smoking ruin of the city sometime after dawn. Coming out of the woods they espied the advance force of Arahaz about a mile distant, guarding the entrance to the valley, one thousand strong under Irdivan.

But Rammeth was brought into the dark holds of Danath Hered before dawn and delivered to the Kushite torturers in the dungeon, who fixed him to a spit and roasted him over a slow fire. In the midst of his agonies he faltered under torment and confessed all he knew to Arahaz. When Arahaz realized that Manissa was close with a mighty host, he was uncertain whether to strengthen his detachment in the valley and give fight to her on open ground or to withdraw his men into the fortress to wait out a siege, and he was unsure of the truthfulness of what Rammeth told him. But Rammeth protested that her force truly was ten thousand strong and that she verily was as close as he had told, so Arahaz gave orders to his captains, saying, "The one thousand men I have posted in the field cannot hold the Asylians out of the valley. Call Irdivan back to the fortress and have all the men take up defensive positions." Thus the order went forth to call the advance force back. Then Rammeth said, "I have done what you willed. I have betrayed my people and delivered them into your hands. Set me free then, to wander in the wilderness as an outcast and lament my wretchedness to the end of my days." But Rammeth was bound hand and foot and taken down into the caverns of Danath Hered, to the putrid chambers which never see light, and there was slain upon the altar of Nergal as a sacrifice.

It was just after dawn when Manissa was watching the

Caeylonics from afar that the order to withdraw reached the thousand men stationed at the foot of the valley, and Naross said, "Look my lady, they are withdrawing!" Amyntas said, "Let us strike them now, before they retreat to their keep! Furthermore, attacking while they withdraw will put them to rout and cause great panic among the Marudans!" Manissa said, "Let it be so, Amyntas, only take not all of our men down there at once, lest our full strength be exposed." So Amyntas took two thousand horsemen of Asylia, and among them was Eridax, to whom he said, "Now is your chance to repair for your folly and avenge your brother's fall."

It was as the sun peaked over the valley of the Cadar and the Caeylonics began their withdrawal towards Danath Hered that Amyntas and the horsemen of Asylia came thundering across the plains hot for blood. The Caeylonic captain Irdivan saw the charge and tried to call his men to order, but only the men closest to the front turned and prepared for battle, while those towards the rear continued their withdrawal, not wanting to be caught in the fight. No matter how much their captains threatened and whipped, they would not be halted, but retreated ever faster, so that the Caeylonic force was depleted by almost half. When the Asylians were almost upon the valley, Irdivan said, "Half of my men have fled; I cannot hold against this force," and ordered his men to retreat. But Amyntas was upon them and rode them down with a great slaughter. Many men were trampled, and those who were not turned and fled, for they perceived the Asylians to be twice their number at least. That day Eridax redeemed himself, for he espied Irdivan the captain in the fray and caught him in his sights, and letting fly his sturdy ashen shaft, a flawless throw, he struck the Caeylonic in the bowels and brought him tumbling from his horse in agony. Thus did Eridax win glory.

But Amyntas rode down the rest of the force, and encircled them with his horses so that they could not return to Danath Hered. Then he and his hardy Asylians hurled their javelins, a rain of doom, and rode in with their whetted swords blazing. They surrounded and corraled the men of Caeylon, hemmed them in like cattle, and slew them like hunters upon the plains surround and slay the great beasts that dwell there. Not a single one among them reached the safety of the fortress, and great and small alike died upon the valley floor. But the head of Irdivan was hurled over the walls of Danath Hered, with a letter reading, "Thus is avenged

Rammeth brother of Eridax, and so shall end Arahaz, stooge of Belthazre."

After this the Asylians encamped around the walls of Danath Hered, so that the Marudans were besieged. Furthermore, many of the refugees from the burning of Cadaras came out of hiding from the woods some distance away and joined Manissa, and another one thousand were added to her ranks in this way. They were organized under Aenon, son-in-law of Garba, and were called the Cadarasian Thousand. Arahaz ordered Danath Hered secured and reinforced the gates. He walked to and fro upon the ramparts, observing the Asylians and pondering what to do, for he was greatly afraid. But Manissa was at a loss as to how to assail the fortress, for as Hadrior said, it was very great, being fifteen feet thick in some places and high enough that no spear throw could reach the men on the battlements. Therefore Manissa sent a message to Arahaz, which said:

Manissa, Maiden and Queen of the Asylians to Arahaz, Captain of the Marudans of Danath Hered-

Though you have dealt treacherously with us in the past by putting to death Ioclus and his house upon the hilltop of Lissus in the wildlands of the north and have acted barbarously in the massacre you have inflicted of late upon Garba and the people of Cadaras, nevertheless we wish to be gracious to you. Therefore, as you see yourself encompassed about and that we are much greater than you, we offer unto you the choice of offering up the fortress freely tomorrow at dawn. If you should do so and choose wisdom over folly, you will be permitted to march home out of Cadarasia into the regions of Caeylon, provided your men swear never to come west again and bear the message to Belthazre thy king that no longer with the Asylians, Cadarasians and peoples of Elabaea tolerate thy tyranny and arrogance. If you refuse these terms, ye shall surely die just as the company of Irdivan was wiped out on the plains before you today to the very last man.

When the message was received, some of the captains of Danath Hered counseled Arahaz to surrender and said that the terms were very generous, but Arahaz pondered them awhile and said, "We

71

know that we serve Belthazre, King of Caeylon, and that even if we were to accept the terms of the Asylians, humiliating though they be, we have not the power to keep them. For Belthazre would no doubt be incensed and command us back to the west again to fight, and how could we resist the will of the king? Or how can we negotiate such a settlement without his leave? Furthermore, if we do give up the fortress and return home, the king will be very wrathful and will execute judgment upon us and put us to miserable deaths. If we leave, it shall certainly go ill for us; but if we stay and fight perhaps we shall prevail. This keep is strong and has stood for many generations. Therefore, my brothers, let us spurn the offer of the Asylians and see what they will bring against us." This counsel seemed good to the Marudans, and so word was sent back to Manissa spurning her terms and declaring that they would remain to the death.

Then Manissa called her captains to her, and with them Aenon, son-in-law of Garba who commanded the Cadarasians, and also Eridax, brother of Rammeth, who had won glory by slaying Irdivan. She related to them how Arahaz had spurned their clemency and had chosen death over surrender and bid them prepare their men for war. The next morning, the Asylians hurled themselves fiercely against Danath Hered but were driven back, for the Marudans rained arrows upon them from the walls and the Asylians were unable to strike back. Some warriors attempted to throw up ladders, but they were hurled down or shot with arrows when they set to climbing them. By midafternoon Amyntas and Arrax pulled the men back with many casualties and said to Manissa, "Though we are many, we have no means to either destroy these walls or to scale them." Manissa brooded in her tent for a time, pondering what course of action to take, when Naross came to speak with her, saying, "There is a man among Aenon's company of Cadarasians who wishes to speak with you." Manissa said, "Show him in." A man was brought in before her, older and worn down with weariness and hardship, but still full of strength and valor.

"May the queen live forever," he said, bowing his head to the floor. Manissa said, "Take heart noble son of Cadarasia. For many generations your people have been of one heart and mind with my own, and your lord Garba was united in the bonds of kinship with my father's house through the marriage of his sister Grianne to my father Ioclus. Therefore, have no fear and speak freely, for I will

72

regard your words as the words of a kinsman. But tell me your name and your father's house." Then the man raised himself and said, "The queen is more gracious than has been told. My name is Aharon, son of Agathon, wretched though I am! I was a merchant in times past and come from a line of merchants and traders, all of whom have dwelt securely in Cadaras until now. When Arahaz marched out against us, my two sons were killed in the citadel with lord Garba, and my wife was slain when the city was burned. I alone have escaped, and now I fight for you, my queen, as the closest living relation to Garba and as the Queen of the Asylians and leader of the Western Tribes."

Manissa smiled gently upon him and said, "The queen is grateful for your service. But what news have you come to tell me that you are brought into my tent after the setting of the sun?" Aharon said, "In the days when I was a merchant, I used to carry goods into Danath Hered for the Caeylonics. In my many journeys into the great fortress, I noticed that in the center of the courtyard there was a vast well, more of a cistern, ten feet wide and three times as many deep. The well drew water from the Cadar for them so that the men of the fortress needed not sally forth outside for fresh water in a time of siege." Manissa said, "I think that would be a bane to us now rather than a boon, do you not think?" Aharon said, "Perhaps, but I know the exact location within the fortress of the cistern -- it is forty paces west of the midpoint of the easternmost wall. Therefore, let the queen send some of her warriors out a ways from the fortress, out of the sight of Arahaz's watchers. There let them dig into the earth and carve out a tunnel in the ground. Run the tunnel under the eastwall of the fortress and in about forty paces, and it should open up into the bottom of the cistern. Then let a troupe of picked men enter the cistern by night, come up it by stealth and throw open the gates to the fortress. In such a manner may we take the fortress of Danath Hered."

Manissa thanked the man and gave him a lionskin valued at two foals for his words. Then she called her lords and explained the plan to them, and they all with one accord thought it good. Arrax was appointed to keep up the attack on the walls of the fortress, so as to distract the Marudans from the digging of the tunnel. Amyntas was placed in charge of the execution of the plan. Therefore, before dawn the next day, Amyntas and five hundred men rode forth about a half mile east from Danath Hered, over the side of a small hillock where they could not be seen from the walls of the keep, and began the work of digging a hole in the earth. Meanwhile, Arrax assaulted the fortress all throughout the day, though with some reserve, as he was only trying to divert attention from the east to the west. When Amyntas and his men returned by cover of night, they told the queen, "We have dug down to a depth of fifteen feet and have made the opening wide enough for three men. The ground is easy and moves before our spades with little effort." Manissa said, "Let it be dug down another ten, and wide enough for four." Thus Amyntas returned the following morning before dawn with his diggers and continued, and that afternoon they ceased digging down and began digging west, and meanwhile Arrax assailed the fortress all that day. They did likewise for six days, and the Caeylonics did not understand what the Asylians were doing, nor did they suspect the scheme of Amyntas. Arahaz boasted, "These foolish barbarians assault the fortress daily, and every day retire without having made any progress. They are like a drunken man who beats his fists on the wall, vainly trying to knock it down!" But everyday Amyntas and his men proceeded closer to the fortress, and each day they carted out a great quantity of dirt, which they carried some distance upstream and began to use to dam the Brook of Cadar. On the seventh day, they dug under the walls of the fortress, and word was brought to Manissa, saying, "By tomorrow evening we shall come upon the cistern."

Manissa then sent Naross and a thousand men east to complete the damming of the Cadar a mile upstream, so that the tunnel would remain dry and the cistern not be full when Amyntas came upon it. Then she told Amyntas to equip each man with a sword and a rope and to prepare to go into the fortress, and told him, "My lord Amyntas, should you succeed in this venture you will be ever in my gratitude." Then she summoned Arrax and said, "Make your attack on the fortress today especially hot, so that we may weary the Marudans." Thus it was that all day long Arrax pestered the defenses of Danath Hered, and though he caused no great damage, he succeeded in irritating the Marudans greatly and wearied them. All the while Amyntas and his men dug towards the cistern, and shortly after nightfall the pick of Amyntas struck the earth and beyond it he felt solid stone. The stone was worked away until a small opening was revealed. Amyntas, with great caution, peered through the hole and saw that they had entered the cistern seven feet from the bottom, and that due to the damming of the Cadar the day before, the water came only to the men's waists.

Then he said, "We shall wait a time until just before the changing of the watch, at the eleventh hour, then we shall make our entry into the well." In the Asylian camp, Manissa hurried with great excitement from tent to tent and told all, "Arm yourselves and be ready to go up and take the fortress, but take care to light no fire, lest we let on that we are preparing for battle."

Thus it was that near midnight of the eighth day of the siege, when the garrison was weary from the day's fighting and the eyes of the watch were heavy, Amyntas and his five hundred picked men came into the bottom of the cistern through the cave they had dug. Some skilled men scaled the walls of the cistern and came forth into the courtyard of the fortress, and finding it deserted, attached many ropes to nearby stones and trees. Thus the men of Amyntas began to climb forth from the cistern. When fifty men had climbed forth with Amyntas, he said, "Steel your spines! Let our arms not fail us now!" He marched them through the courtyard to the gates, which they found guarded by two dozen men. Amyntas said, "Everybody pick your man, for we shall strike but once!" Because it was dark and close to the time of the changing of the watch, the guards thought that Amyntas and the Marudans were their comrades there to relieve them, and they spoke to them in a friendly manner. But when they approached and saw their long hair, they cried, "Elabaeans!" and took up their swords. But the men of Amyntas came upon them and struck them with their swords, each one killing his man. Nevertheless, the guards upon the walls perceived what was going on, and hearing the cries of their comrades, raised the alarm. Then Amyntas said, "We are discovered! Let us fling this gate open before we die!" So all of the men tore off the barricades from the gates and pushed them open.

Naross was stationed near the entrance of the fortress, waiting to call the attack. He heard the clamor, then saw the gates open, and then perceived Amyntas standing in the gateway with sword raised. His old blood boiled hot, and he cried, "The fortress is taken! Amyntas has thrown open the gates!" Then all of the Asylians charged forth from their tents with spears in hand and shields sparkling in the starlight, and some on horseback. Manissa herself mounted Ruah her horse and took the lead, crying, "Now drive the foreigner from our land!"

Before the Marudans could rally a defense, the Asylians were upon the gates. The men of Amyntas continued to pour forth from the cistern until all five hundred were accounted for and ran throughout the pathways slaying the guards they came upon. Word was brought to Arahaz of the breach, and he came to the balcony overlooking the courtyard. There he saw the Asylians pouring in the gates, charging the ramparts and hurling the guardsmen from the walls. In the courtyard he saw the Marudans and Asylians locked in bitter combat, with Manissa herself on horseback riding to and fro, striking all in her path with the massive spear of Ioclus, cleaving flesh and smashing bone and leaving a trail of death in her wake. There was Arrax, bringing doom wherever he went and routing Marudans before him. Lo! Amyntas, fierce lord of Kerion, led his men thoughout the buildings, setting fire to them and putting Caeylonics to the sword. Naross took a thousand men and stormed the nether regions of the fortress, freeing prisoners, slaying men and rampaging until they came to the Temple of Nergal with its bronze idol, which they hurled down and broke in pieces. Hadrior, Eridax and Aenon with his Cadarasian Thousand raged here and there, engaging the Marudans hotly. One of the captains of Maruda came running up to Arahaz and said, "My lord! They have taken all of the battlements and are prevailing everywhere! What shall we do?" Arahaz scowled and said, "Do whatever seems best to you. Is it not clear that the fortress is lost?" Then Arahaz fled to his quarters and called his servants to him. He hid inside a basket and had them lower him through an outside window by several ropes. When he reached the ground, he took to his heels and fled into the woods, thus cheating death for a time.

But the Elabaeans continued the pillage and slaughter throughout the night and did not restrain their fury until the rising of the sun. When light came and they beheld the destruction they had wrought, Naross said, "Now are Ioclus and Garba avenged." Then Manissa came forth from the smoking battlements and cried victory, and all the Cadarasians and Asylians bowed and did homage to her. She seemed glorious in that moment, illumined by the rising sun, her form both beautiful and terrible to behold with her gore-covered spear in one hand and her long hair blowing upon the spring wind. Then the Asylians came forth from the fortress and gathered together and found that they had taken two thousand prisoners and had slain nigh unto four thousand men. Besides these, they also found within the fortress some eight hundred Asylian women who had been captured and were at the time awaiting removal to Caeylon. They also had taken booty equal to fifty bars of gold, as they are reckoned in Caeylon. Thus there was much rejoicing in the fall of Danath Hered, the hated emblem of Marudan tyranny, and great excitement over the treasures that fell into Asylian hands.

Chapter 9
The Coming of Adaran

After the Asylians were in command of Danath Hered, an argument arose in the camp about whether to occupy the fortress or to pull it down, and what to do with the prisoners. Hadrior was of the opinion that Danath Hered should be kept and manned by Asylians and Cadarasians as an outpost against Caeylonic invasion and as something to bargain with Belthazre over. But Amyntas mocked him and said, "This makes no sense however one looks at it. This fortress is far from our homeland; how can we possibly keep it garrisoned and safe? Furthermore, it is not the way of the Elabaeans to fight from inside walls, but to range openly across the plains. And what is your bargain you propose? Shall we give back to Belthazre what so many have died to overthrow?" Thus there was a fierce dissention between them, with some taking one side, some another. Then Manissa said, "Naross, uncle and wisest among us, what say you?" Naross said, "My lady, if we choose to retain this fortress, nothing good can come of it, for the Marudans may come upon us and retake it, strenthen it and oppress us even worse. As the noble and renowned Amyntas said, such is not the way of the peoples of the west. Therefore let it be torn down." So Manissa gave the command and all of the hosts of Asylia and Cadarasia were set to work pulling down the fortress.

But meanwhile Arrax was wrathful against many of his captains who had taken prisoners, hoping to ransom them for gold. He berated them, and said, "Shall you sheath your vengeful swords for the hope of some pieces of Marudan gold? Have we not pledged to drown Caeylon in blood? Do you not know these men will only return to fight you another day?" Then he said to the prisoners, "I give you no word of safety, for these men who have taken you under their protection have done so without my leave." But Manissa said, "Arrax, most lordly and powerful of all the captains here, your prowess in war and cunning in the assembly are not in question. But what valor can there be in putting a thousand prisoners to death who have surrendered themselves willingly? Though your captains acted without leave, we are bound in honor to abide by their word. The prisoners shall not die. Yet neither shall they be ransomed, lest it be said that the Asylians can be bought with gold. They shall be taken inland, into the wilds of Asylia, and be put to labor there until such a time when the fighting ends and they can be safely returned." Arrax bowed to her, and the Caeylonic prisoners prostrated themselves before Manissa and said, "Rightly do they speak well of you, lady Manissa, for thou art fierce in battle and clement in victory!"

It took the Asylians near a month to dismantle the fortress. But they were not idle, for detachments were sent out under Arrax and Aenon, son-in-law of Garba, and the Asylians struck the other smaller fortresses that ringed in the land of Cadarasia. Arrax pushed northward, stricking the stronghold of Debir with the edge of the sword and burned it and put its garrison to death, three hundred men in all. Then he turned towards the borders of Epidymia and struck the fortified city of Tunon with the edge of the sword. The garrison took refuge inside a mighty tower, but Arrax set fire to it and thus killed those who were within. The tower and walls were destroyed, and five hundred men were slain in all. Then he rode northeast and attacked Kephtor and struck it with the edge of the sword. The walls were breached and the fighting was thick, and in the midst of the fray Arrax was struck with a Marudan spear in the shoulder and fell. But his captains resumed the fighting and took the fortress and put the garrison to the sword, two hundred fifty men in all. Arrax was carried in a litter back to the camp at Cadaras and treated.

Aenon won glory in the south, for he led his Cadarasian Thousand forth and struck An Dara with the edge of the sword and burned it, slaying four hundred Marudans. Then he turned and struck the fortress of Ehuiel and destroyed it and put the men of the garrison to death, some three hundred fifty men. But he dallied too long in plundering Ehuiel, and the men of the southernmost fortress of Neboran heard of the fall of Ehuiel and sallied forth from the fortress, five hundred in all. They surprised Aenon at the ruins of Ehuiel and engaged him there, and the Marudan charioteers rode down the Asylians and slew a great number of them. Aenon himself was hit with an arrow in the neck and perished. But his men retreated and formed up on the plain and marching south against Neboran stormed it with a great fury. The garrison of the fortress surrendered, but the men of Aenon, wrathful at the death of their captain, took them to the nearby cliffs and hurled them forth so that they were dashed upon the crags of the valley floor. When all this was accomplished, word was brought back to Manissa that the Caeylonics had been utterly stomped out of the land and put to death and all of their strongholds were destroyed.

Then Manissa said, "We have turned the east into a region of blood and fire and wailing. Let us return now to the west, to the green fields of Asylia and the fires of the Hall of Orix. Perhaps the Marudans will leave us in peace now." So the Asylians struck camp at the start of the second month since the overthrow of Danath Hered and returned forthwith to the west, crossing over the Erriad on Midsummer's Eve and returning again into Asylia. But many of the men of Cadaras left her and remained behind in the east to rebuild the City on the Plain.

Yet in Caeylon there was great unrest, even in the very palace of Belthazre. Caravans brought back word of the loss of Danath Hered, and soon reports came of the overthrow of all of the other Caeylonic outposts in the west. Most of all were the people amused at the expense of Arahaz, whose escape in a basket became well known throughout the city. And a great mockery was made of Arahaz. Thus it was that Arahaz, after fleeing east for many days, had taken up a disguise with a caravan he ran in with and came into the city secretly, fearing what Belthazre would do if he were discovered. Therefore he did not go to Belthzare, but instead presented himself at the quarters of the Queen Narússa, still in disguise. The eunuchs of the queen went to fetch her and said, "There is a merchant at the gate to see you." Narússa went out to meet him and recognized Arahaz at once. She began to laugh, saying, "My lord Arahaz, where is your uniform? Have you become a dealer in fine clothes? Perhaps that was the meaning behind the basket!" Arahaz bowed and said, "My lady, I must speak with you, for the matter is quite urgent."

Narússa's countenance fell. "Do not tell me about urgent matters," she scowled. Word has reached the city of your shameful defeat, the loss of Danath Hered and the overthrow of our presence in the west, and the king is apt to hold me responsible! It was I who goaded Belthazre the king to treat the Asylians with such a heavy hand. By the gods, he was prepared to make peace with them after the revolt of Ioclus! Now in the past nine months he has lost nigh on nine thousand men in this western wilderness trying to pacify these barbarians, and it is I whom he holds responsible. Daily I tremble for my life, for who can restrain the king when he rages in anger?"

Arahaz said, "And has he spoken of me?" Narússa replied, "He has called you craven and vowed to hang you." Arahaz said, "Though he slay me, yet will I go in to him. I have always been able to turn away his wrath face-to-face. Who knows? Perhaps I shall yet live. I will take off my rainment and come before him in sackcloth. Perhaps I shall move him to pity." Narússa laughed and said, "Or perhaps you shall die. And then his wrath will be satisfied and turn away from me." Arahaz bowed and said, "The queen is compassionate and merciful." Then he took his leave and went to seek an audience with Belthazre.

Now Belthazre was making his monthly offerings in the temple of the goddess Innana for the fertility of his house when word was brought to him that Arahaz had presented himself in the main chamber. Then Belthazre was filled with rage and dropped the cup of libation which he meant to offer, spilling the wine upon the pavement. He stormed about the palace in a rage, cursing Arahaz and seeking him that he might put him to death. But when Belthazre entered the chamber, Arahaz prostrated himself on the floor and did obesciance, and the king saw his sackcloth and ashes and the leg, crippled by the spear of Ioclus, and was moved to pity for him. Then his rage left him, and the king said, "Arise, Arahaz." And Arahaz arose before the King of Caeylon. Then Belthazre sent him away with his eunuchs, to be bathed and arrayed in fine clothes that he might again appear before him.

Then Arahaz was brought into the chambers of Belthazre and feasted with the king, but he still trembled and was afraid to speak. Finally Belthazre said, "Arahaz, though your failures merit death, I do not hold you accountable for what has occured as of late in Elabaea. It was my wife Narússa who has brought all this upon me. She envied the delight of my eyes when I would have possessed the maid Eilia for my harem and had her slain. It was she who counseled me to send you orders to arrest Ioclus and make war upon the Asylians. It was by her foul tongue that I took a heavy hand with this Manissa and compelled you to send Tegleth into the west, and to lay waste to Cadarasia. By all the gods, when these affairs are settled I shall deal with her! But these things have stirred fire in their hearts, and it shall not be put out now save by drenching it in blood." Arahaz said, "What does the king propose?" Then Belthazre said, "From the death of my father Dathan until this day I have cared little for the doings in the west. I have filled my days in luxury and idleness about the palace, allowing the Asylians

81

to wax strong. Now I see my folly in this. Yet from this day forward have I made a vow that I shall divert all my energies to the subduction of Elabaea, the slaughter of the Asylians and the conquest of the west."

Arahaz said, "My king, great are your words and grand your designs! I have seen the Elabaeans near me, even at my door, and can give the king much counsel on how best to make war upon them." Belthazre laughed and said, "Your arrogance in presuming to advise the king would be a serious offense if it were not rendered so laughable by your recent disastrous defeat at the hands of the very Asylians whom you propose to tell me how to subdue! No, for this task I have another in mind, a general of proven merit and blood relation to my father's house. I speak of Adaran of Gontras. I am even now assembling an army greater than any that has ridden forth out of Caeylon since the days of Anathar. Two thousand chariots and many more thousand foot soldiers armed with new brazen shields and spears, each experienced in war. It is my will to empty Maruda of every able bodied soldier and send them forth into the west for the destruction of the Elabaeans. The end of Adaran's invasion will be the utter destruction of all the Elabaeans, every man, woman and child, the young with the old. I grow weary of this quarrelsome people and would clear them from the lands west of Cadaras that we might dwell there and encircle the Epidymians from the south. Adaran has fought and slew many men of Epidymia, and in comparison the men of Asylia will be as lambs to the slaughter."

Arahaz said, "What does my king wish of me?" Belthazre said, "You shall accompany Adaran, but shall not command. You shall ride with him and do his bidding and serve him in whatever he says, yet you shall be under him and in no way presume to advise him unless bidden. When he goes into the west, you will go by his side, and to atone for your failures you will either kill Manissa or yourself be killed by the Asylians. I have spared you this day, but do not dare to return to me again unless you can bring me word that Manissa is dead." Then he dismissed Arahaz and sent him to the quarters of Adaran, who was encamped without the city on the south going towards Gontras. From that day forward Arahaz dwelt with Adaran and was forbidden to go elsewhere but where Adaran gave him leave, a period of two years.

This Adaran was a distant kinsman of Belthazre, a general since the time of Dathan and the victor of many battles with the

Epidymians, whom nobody until his time had been able to defeat. Therefore he was arrogant and boasted that he would make a complete end of Manissa and the Asylians. But he bided his time and dwelt in Caeylon for over a year provisioning his army, training and making ready for the campaign west. He tarried for a long while in Caeylon supplying his army with provisions, drilling his men and learning about the ways of the Asylians from other men who had spent much time in the west. But Arahaz he despised, and though he treated him well and alloted him several servants to wait upon him, he did not call for him or seek his counsel in any of his deliberations, nor inform him of his plans. But the advisor of Adaran, a man named Bula of great wisdom and counsel, befriended Arahaz and brought him news of all that was done by Adaran in preparation for the campaign.

But Manissa returned to the city of Asylia in great splendor shortly after Midsummer after departing Cadaras. She took her place in the Hall of Orix and sat upon the throne of Ioclus and held counsel with her lords. Many Cadarasians from the outlying villages and settlements which had been deserted or burned by Arahaz fled west and took refuge in Asylia, men from Avlos, Elos and the region around Cadarasia. King Endumion of Cyrenaica also jounreyed to the Hall of Orix and pledged loyalty to Manissa and the house of Ioclus, as did many of the chieftains of the Iturs to the north. The Lugarians did not pledge fealty to Manissa, but sent emissaries promising aid if they were called upon and swore an oath of friendship to her house forever. Having thus destroyed Danath Hered and made alliances with many of the tribes of Elabaea, Manissa summoned grey-headed Naross and said to him, "Uncle, who are both wise and mighty, throughout our campaigns I have been troubled by the thought of my father, noble Ioclus, and the rest of my kin, who lay in shallow graves upon the top of the hill of Lissus in the wild northlands. Tender Osseia, fierce Menelor and innocent Saraeth! They rot in unmarked graves, the prey of beasts and scavengers. Therefore, as the second eldest after my father, you shall take a company and return to Lissus. Search the oak grove and recover the bodies of our kin and bring them hither." Thus Naross took forty men and made a journey to the north, to the place in the wilds where Manissa had specified, and they found the hill by reason of the bleached bones of the slain men of Caeylon which lay exposed upon the hillside. Upon reaching the oaks, they put their spades to the earth and came upon the remains of the house of Ioclus, and accounted for all of them. But the body of Gygas, which Manissa had left to moulder where it fell, Naross did not find. Then Naross cleansed the bones and interred them in three urns, one for Ioclus, one for the children of Ioclus, and one for the servants of Ioclus. Then these were brought back to Asylia with much pomp and ceremony, and the people came forth from the city and wept while the procession wound its way up the road into the city. But Manissa told Naross, "Of all people my mother, Grianne, was most beloved by my father, and she lies entombed in the ruins of Cadaras, near her kin and the house of Garba. Therefore, make haste back to Cadaras and inter my father's remains there by those of my mother." Naross did as Manissa commanded, but the bones of Masaros, Menelor, Eleth, Saraeth and Osseia, as well as the servants, were interred in Asylia.

Then Manissa held counsel as the leaves began to fall throughout Elabaea and said, "Who will go up against the Marudans?" Eridax and Amyntas said, "We will!" Then they went out with companies and made war upon the Marudans who dwelt in the eastern marches of Elabaea. Sometimes they raided caravans who had come to trade for horses, and other times they burned settlements that the people of Caeylon had made. Many of the Marudans banded together, and soldiers from Caeylon came at times, and the Asylians and Marudans engaged in pitched battles. Sometimes the Asylians triumphed and drove the Marudans from the field, and other times the Marudans triumphed and put the Asylians to rout, slaying a great number of them. Not a few Marudans, who had lived in Elabaea for sometime and were accustomed to its ways, made their way to Asylia and did homage to Manissa and asked to be put under the rule of the Asylians, whom they had found to be much more just and equitable than the rule of the Marudans; and as many who did so were received as compatriots by Manissa. Thus the regions east of the Erriad were full of raids, ambushes and burnings all throughout that autumn and into the following spring. The east was in disarray, but Cadaras had been rebuilt and populated again by the following summer. But the entire house of Garba was fallen, for when Aenon son-in-law or Garba had perished at Ehuiel, the house of Garba was left without an heir. Therefore the Cadarasians sent emissaries to Manissa to ask her counsel in the matter, and she sent unto them Eridax, in whom she now had great confidence, and gave him in marriage to Danica, one of the nieces of Garba, and said, "Eridax shall rule Cadarasia as its lord, but shall remain tributary to Asylia insofar as he is one of our people." Thus were the peoples of Asylia and Cadarasia united in the marriage of Eridax to Danica, and thereafter the two nations were regarded as one people, and Manissa claimed authority of all the lands from the Cyrian Highlands and the border of Lugaria eastward across the Erriad to Cadarasia and the boundaries of Caeylon and as far north as the wildlands of Thon and the southern marches of Epidymia. To the south her kingdom stretched to the foothills of the Bados Mountains, which were unpopulated except for the wildmen who dwell there.

And during those months Manissa waxed strong and made war on the Marudans, raiding their caravans and plundering their settlements in the region south of Cadarasia and eastward as far as the marches of Anentora where one comes into the domain of Caeylon. So frequent were their raids that in that year the Marudan horse merchants ceased coming into Elabaea and many Caeylonic settlers and traders fled back into the east. But many who were of sterner mind banded together and took to the countryside in hopes of laying an ambush for the Asylians or in some way striking against them. And the whole land was filled with the burning of wagons, the flight of exiles and the cries of battle in the bitter winter. Manissa was brought word in the Hall of Orix, "Everywhere our riders strike at the Caeylonics, but they are fierce and fight us with vigor and we have yet to drive them from the land."

But by and by spring came and the snows melted, and Adaran made ready his forces On the full moon of the fifth month, as the wet spring settled into a dry summer, Adaran assembled his hosts on the plains outside Caeylon and marshalled his forces for war. Belthazre came forth from his palace with his entourage, dressed splendidly in robes of azure silk embroidered with gold, the train of which was five cubits in length and was carried by several attendants. Thus attired he took his seat upon the walls of the city by the western gate to observe the army of Adaran. Narússa his wife came forth as well, born aloft in a litter by Kushite servants and watching from afar.

Never was so mighty an army assembled from the time of Anathar even unto that day! Who was among that host that stood before the glimmering walls of Caeylon that day, so splendind and so ill-fated? First among them all was Adaran, the kinsman of

Belthazre the king, who had won glory against the Epidymians. Glorious was his rainment, for he was covered in gleaming bronze armor from head to foot, marvelously wrought by the craftsmen of king, and upon it carved with a multitude of figures of beasts, flowering plants and warriors. On his head was a great warhelm of finely hammered bronze gilded with silver and gold with the seal of the house of Anathar upon the crest. He bore at his side a great scimitar and carried also a mighty spear, Lysonian in origin, measuring five cubits and capped with a brazen tip whetted to a fine edge. About his shoulders he donned a great red cloak. Thus attired he stood upon his chariot car, his servant Bula beside him, and with a great voice called to King Belthazre upon the walls and said, "Behold the armies of the king!"

Yet who else was among that great host? First among them was Keniah, a great warrior from Caeylon, who bore a bronze shield overlaid with four layers of hide which he had won in battle from a Vecantian giant; he was set over a thousand. In the wars against the men of Vecanti he had slain a hundred men, and after Adaran he was feared the most by the foes of Caeylon. Among the charioteers were two brothers, Zimrah and Eluah, archers both, whose arrows were death-bringing and whose aim failed never. Also in the number of Adaran was a spearman of the Baazites, Omer the Fast. This Omer was a kinsman of Tegleth (whom Arrax slew) and the swiftest runner among all the men of Maruda, for he alone of all men had once outrun an Elabaean charger in a wager and won fame by this deed, and greatly to be dreaded was the cast of his spear. And Omer was set over a multitude as well. Also among the army of Adaran were others of great repute: Mozarus of Nadare and Enech of Lyson, men of renown; Nabuzar, Andarat, Polassur and Zeleth, all men of Caeylon; Anurah, Olrath and Negurac, all Kushite warriors of great fame. Thus the army of Adaran was arrayed upon the plain, marshalled according to their thousands and according to their hundreds, with captains set over all. Then the trumpet blast was given, and hundreds upon hundreds of horns resounded throughout the ranks, announcing the setting forth of the grand army of Adaran on the fifteenth day of the fifth month in the third year of the reign of Belthazre, being the second year of the reign of Manissa.

First of all were arrayed the glorious two thousand chariots of Adaran, all new and glittering in the bright sun of Maruda, led by the strong steeds of Elabaea. Behind them marched the great

86

multitudes of spearmen, arranged in companies of hundreds and marching rank on rank, each bearing their ensign and standard and led by men skilled in warfare and manuevers, ten thousand strong. Then rode the cavalry and the scouts, mounted units who were equipped to ride fast and far; they numbered three thousand. Finally came the supply trains, wagons and caravans bearing thousands of cartloads of provisions for the mighty host. Many merchants, traders and craftsmen also followed in the train of Adaran's army, for they hoped to be allowed to again trade freely in Elabaea or even to dwell there after the Asylians were dispossessed, and many brought their entire families in the caravans with the intent of settling in Elabaea. Thus there were a great number of women and children in the rear of the host, and the number of the merchants, craftsmen, traders and their families was not less than five thousand. Besides these were many other useless fellows, men who had been imprisoned for debt, or rabble from the cities who had been promised pay to go forth with Adaran, and they numbered some four thousand. Thus all the men of Caeylon who marched west with Adaran were nigh unto twenty five thousand persons who drew the sword, not counting the tradesmen and women. Belthazre blessed them from the gates of the city, and the priests of Caeylon offered up sacrifices to Adar, the patron god of Adaran. Belthazre said, "This army goes forth to the glory of Caeylon and the renown of my house forever." But Narússa, watching from the shade of her canopy, scoffed and said, "This is an army of fools, and their own folly will be the undoing."

The army of Adaran took one month to progress westward to the marches of Anentora by the plains betwixt Caeylon and Cadarasia, by virtue of its great multitude and the great number of merchants and women trailing behind. When they had crossed into Elabaea and marched for three days, Adaran pitched his camp at the place called An Danara, about a four day journey east of Cadarasia. Then he sent out riders to scout the lands as far as Cadaras and report on the movements of the Asylians, ordering them to return by Midsummer Eve, a little over a fortnight hence. Then the Marudans settled down to eat, drink and play. But Arahaz was shunned by Adaran and his advisors, save for Bula, chief advisor of Adaran, who was very wise. Then Bula came unto the tent of Arahaz by night and said to him, "Is it well with you, my lord Arahaz?" Arahaz said, "It is well. Enter and drink wine with me." So the two reclined in the tent of Arahaz and drank wine and talked into the night.

Arahaz said, "Master Bula, your lord Adaran knows not the temperment of the Asylians. They will not risk defeat by engaging him in open war like this, for they always work by trickery and deceit." Bula said, "Was it the deceit of the Asylians which gave to you that wound upon your leg that cripples you and has driven you forever from the battlefield?" Arahaz scoffed and said, "This wound was given to me by Ioclus, lord of Asylia, on the night I surrounded his camp to take his life. On that night it was we who behaved with treachery, seducing Gygas the Gelan to betray his lord. But curse that day! Curse the day that Gygas came seeking me, and the day that I pressed hard upon the oak covered slope of Lissus thinking to end there forever the arrogance of the barbarian peoples of this wretched land! On that night was unleashed a torrent of blood that has cost me dear and has yet to be staunched. The Asylians took to the wilderness and struck us wherever they could. They routed my most powerful captain and slew him, then gained entry into Danath Hered by stealth and threw it to the ground. Then they went throughout the land and struck all of our fortifications and towers and put the garrisons to death. When you have them in your eye with your spear ready to cast, it is then that the Asylian withdraws. But when you lean upon your spear in slothfulness, weary at your watch, then they come forth and strike! Adaran, thy master, will hunt them in vain. And she who eluded me on Lissus' muddy slopes will come for him in the dark."

Bula said, "Are you that bitter from the wound given to you by Ioclus that you wish disaster upon our kinsmen?" Arahaz said, "I wish no ill upon any man, but I foresee in Adaran the same foolhardiness with which I approached these Asylians two years prior, and for which I have payed dearly. Caeylon and our Lord Belthazre could be strengthened more by allying with Manissa and the Elabaeans than by making war upon them. Then trade could resume and Caeylon could turn its eye elsewhere." Thus they spoke far into the night, Arahaz predicting ruin for the expedition and Bula contesting him.

But meanwhile the scouts of Adaran reached the hills around Cadarasia and saw that the city was weak and ill defended, for it had not yet been rebuilt from the overthrow of Arahaz. They pressed on to the northwest, into the wildlands east of the Erriad, and found the countryside at peace, the Elabaeans dwelling securely in their villages and the horses roaming freely upon the

88

plain. Then they returned to Adaran with haste and said, "Behold! The gods have delivered the Elabaeans into your hand, for the whole countryside is at rest and the city of Cadaras is ill-defended." Then Adaran rejoiced and roused the army and all the chariots and said, "Forth to war! We will chasten these barbarians!" Then he brought forth the entire might of his hosts to the plains of Cadaras, leaving none behind, in order to frighten the Cadarasians and strike panic into Elabaea.

But Eridax, lord of Cadaras, was not caught unawares, for some shepherds had ventured east with their flocks and spied the Caeylonic army from over the hillocks and returned briskly to Eridax with word of the coming of Adaran. Then Eridax sent his wife and all of the women and children with the elderly out of Cadaras to the west, over the Erriad to Manissa's country and fair Asylia in hopes of finding refuge there. Then he gathered about him every man who could swing a sword or shoot a bow, three thousand in all, and said to them, "We will not be penned in here and suffer the same fate as Garba of happy memory. Danath Hered is destroyed and our walls are being rebuilt, but we have neither the fortifications nor the men to withstand a siege. Therefore, let every man mount his horse and ride with me into battle upon the plains. There we will meet the Marudans and crush them or be smashed against them." Then all of the Cadarasians cried, "Cru Cadara!" which was the warcry of that noble people. So each man, led by Eridax, mounted their steeds and came forth from the city by night.

Then one of the scouts of Eridax came and said, "The army of Caeylon moves west from An Danara and is immense indeed. They are but a half-night's ride from here." So Eridax and his riders pressed across the plains with the foothills of Bados flying by them on the south all that evening, and at sunrise came upon Adaran four leagues west of An Danara. The Caeylonics were somewhat in disarray, having just switched their watch. Some of the soldiers were up and in formation, but others were raising from sleep, and many of the charioteers were absent. Then someone gave the cry that the Elabaeans were upon them, and Adaran blew the battle trumpet.

The riders of Cadaras lowered their spears, their eyes filled with fire and the wind behind their steeds. Thus they came crashing into the lines of the Marudans and trampelled a great number underfoot and slew many, casting deadly spears this way and that; as many as were caught in their aim were pierced and fell upon the dusty plain. But the Caeylonics were not idle, and Adaran gave the commands to his captains to encircle the Elabaeans. Then the infantry, led by Keniah, backed away from Eridax and formed up around him in a great circle, so that the horsemen of Cadarasia were hemmed in by spears on all sides. Then Eridax perceived his folly in charging the Marudans so rashly, seeing that they were of much greater numbers than he had thought, and that the Cadarasians were penned in with no escape. The men of Maruda hurled their spears, fired their arrows and slung stones at the horsemen as they circled about the field in search of a point to break out, but none was found. Adaran gave the command and the Caeylonics tightened the circuit about them, so they had little room to ride and the barrage of missiles and stones grew very thick. The sturdy horses of Elabaea began to pant, then men were panic-stricken, and many began to fall. Adaran perceived their rout and ordered Keniah to come forward with his infantry and make an end of the Cadarasians, and he fell upon them with a great slaughter. But Eridax fled with but a single warrior, Karyon by name, and fought his way out of the melee to the plains. They rode west in haste, wearied with grief and stricken with many wounds.

Chapter 10
The Flight of the Asylians

After the battle, Adaran gazed out upon the field of Cadarasians lying dead and dying with their horses beside them. He summoned Arahaz to his side and said, "Do you see this sight Arahaz? Behold, the Elabaeans have charged us thinking to break our ranks but have instead gone down to ruin. Are these corpses upon the grass the bodies of the same men who overthrew Danath Hered and slew Tegleth the Baazite?" Arahaz said, "They charged you thus only because of their folly and because Manissa was not with them.Yet be wary, for they are cunning." But Adaran scoffed and derided Arahaz in sight of the other officers and sent him away. So Arahaz went back to his tents and brooded.

But Eridax and Karyon rode swiftly and pressed on without rest until they crossed the Erriad. There they paused but for a moment and continued on again for three days until they entered the region of Asylia and the Hall of Orix where Manissa sat enthroned. As they rode upon the gates, hoary-headed Naross spied them and called out, "Lo, what good word from the Lord of Cadaras?" But then he saw that Eridax was distressed and fatigued and so led him and Karyon inside and refreshed them and let them rest. When they were thus rested, they were summoned to Manissa's presence and came in before her and beheld her. She sat upon the throne of her father cloaked in green, her golden tresses falling upon her shoulders, one hand extended clasping the spear of Ioclus and the other hand resting delicately upon her lap. Then Eridax said, "Hail, Queen of Elabaea!" and did obeisance to her.

Manissa smiled upon him and said, "Grace to you Eridax, Lord of Cadaras. What matter is so pressing that you ride three days without rest to stand in my hall?" Then Eridax told her of the coming of Adaran and of the destruction of his own men and of the size and makeup of the Marudan army. Hadrior, who stood near the throne of Manissa, said, "Curse you Eridax for your recklessness in charging the Caeylonics thus! Did you not do the same before the battle of Danath Hered when your premature attack cost your brother his life? Now your rash deeds have brought forth the ruin of your people." At this Eridax was very wroth with Hadrior, but did not remonstrate with him at that time out of respect for the queen.

But Manissa said, "Thy deeds indeed were rash, young Eridax, for now the Caeylonics will think we are weakened and easily beaten and will be heartened to pursue us farther into the west. And what are we to do?" Hadrior said, "My lady, why not send forth swift riders to the east to see if what Eridax says has truly come to pass and whether or not this Adaran is truly moving against us?" Manissa said, "Let it be so," and three riders were sent forth with utmost haste to the east to bring back word of Adaran's movements.

At that very time Adaran had already set his army moving again, for his advisor Bula said, "This victory has panicked them and brought fear upon their ranks. Let us press our victory and turn it into a rout." So the army of Adaran marched westward, its multitudes covering the fair plains from the fields of Cadaras even to the horizon and sending forth a mighty cloud of dust as they moved. To what can the marching of the men be likened? Lo, they were like a moving forest, the men with their spears held aloft by their hundreds and their thousands. Their feet trampled the earth and made dust where there was grass, and the pleasant streamlets and rills of that land were given over for drink to the soldiers and their beasts and left behind dry when the army passed. The heads of the brazen spears, the polished shields and the embossed chariots all glittered white in the sun of the noon, so that no man standing upon the highlands could bear to look at the army of Adaran lest he be blinded by the reflection. The din and roar of the army was great while it moved across the countryside, like the sound of the crashing of the ocean or the roaring blast of the tempest. Behind the army came the great multitude of wagons, camels, merchants, servants and others who were like a mass of ants upon the earth.

Thus did the three riders of Manissa sight the army of Adaran as it moved west from Cadaras, a two day ride east of Erriad. As their eyes roamed about the plains from the top of one of the many hillocks in the region of Dar Epha, they sighted a great cloud of dust moving upon the western horizon. They rode east with haste and came within sight of the army, where they could make out the standards of Maruda and see the glimmering of the spearheads in the sun. Then they said, "Eridax has not misspoken, for this is without doubt the greatest army that has ever come into

Elabaea. The land is destroyed just by the passing of it." So they turned their steeds west and pressed on with great trepidation, passing back over the Erriad into Asylia and returning to the Hall of Orix within four days and reporting to Manissa all they had seen.

In the meantime, Manissa had summoned the lords of Elabaea to her hall: Naross of the Great Throw; noble Amyntas of Kerion, first in the eyes of Manissa; sharp-tongued Hadrior, brother-in-law of Manissa; rash Eridax, lord of Cadarasia; and hot-blooded Arrax, uncle of the queen and of all the lords of Elabaea the most deadly. Also summoned were ambassadors from the King of Cyrenaica and the lords of Ituria, as well as some of the free tribes of Lugaria. She said to them, "Our peril is most severe. Our scouts tell us that the army of Adaran is greater than any host that has walked the earth since Anathar, and that they swallow up all in their path. This time Belthazre has sent forth the bulk of his army and they come to annihilate. Furthermore, they will be over the Erriad and into Asylia within seven days. What shall be done?"

Then was there a bitter dispute in the Hall of Orix, for some of the party of Arrax said that they ought to be attacked with whatever forces the queen could muster before they passed the Erriad and came into Asylia, but others said that it would be foolish to put the Caeylonic army to the front and the river to the rear of the Asylian force. Amyntas and Naross, on the other hand, said that they should follow the course laid down by Ioclus some years earlier: that Asylia should be abandoned and Manissa make for the wilderness. There she could draw the Elabaeans to herself and attack Adaran only when the time was right. But Manissa said, "Let us not forget that the last time this was attempted, we were betrayed by Gygas the Accursed and the whole house of Ioclus was slain, save myself only." Hadrior argued that even now peace could be made between Asylia and Maruda, and that Manissa ought to cede all of the lands east of the Erriad to Adaran, but he was violently shouted down by the others, who clashed their spears on the shields and called him a coward. But Manissa said, "Brother, Belthazre has gone to great lengths to assemble this army, and nothing short of our blood will stop it." So they debated for some time about what was to be done.

Finally, Manissa stood up tall and glorious and clasped the spear of Ioclus, and the hall fell silent. Then she said, "This I propose. We cannot defeat Adaran as he is now, for his numbers are too great and his supplies too many. Therefore, let us abandon Asylia and strike forth into the wilderness, though not to flee but to ensnare this arrogant Marudan. We shall make a feint and draw Adaran west, allowing him to take Asylia and encouraging him in pursuit. We will stay only a few days ahead of him and move briskly, causing him to march with great haste, for he will imagine that he has routed us. But we shall draw him west, and thus thin out his supply lines so that he can no longer provide for his massive host. We will numerous times fall almost within his grasp and then withdraw, leaving him ever more eager to pursue and ever more certain that he will return to Caeylon in glory. Thus we will draw him deep into the wilderness, beyond Asylia, out into the highlands and even beyond, to the regions where the riders of Asylia have never ventured. When we have exhausted him with much marching into a distant and strange land, we will thus ensnare him, cut off his supplies and smash their armies at our leisure, crushing the pride of Caeylon and dealing Belthazre a blow from which he shall never recover. Then ever after will Asylia be free from the hand of Maruda."

When the lords of Asylia heard the words of Manissa, they shouted and crashed their spears to their shields in approval, but the emissaries of the King of Cyrenaica said, "This goes beyond the aid we have come to give, and we will not support you in this venture." Then the lords grew wroth with them and seized them and treated them roughly. Arrax said, "My queen, let us put these ambassadors to the sword, for they have heard our plans and now desire to return back to their king after vowing not to help us! What is to stop them from betraying all to the Caeylonics?" Manissa said, "Set them loose uncle! Though the Cyrenaicans may disagree with us on strategy, they are no foes of ours and do not wish the Marudan in their land any more than we do in ours. But, men of Cyrenaica, Arrax is correct; you cannot be allowed to destroy our plans the way the plans of Ioclus were destroyed by Gygas. Therefore you will be escorted back to Cyrenaica by some of my riders, and any Cyrenaican henceforth caught coming south along the Itur trail will be slain." So the Cyrenaicans were freed and sent home in the custody of Karyon, the friend of Eridax who had proven his bravery by fighting his way through Adaran's warriors. But the Cyrenaicans were bitter in their heart and meditated on how they could injure Manissa.

That very day the word went forth throughout Asylia and all

its environs that Manissa was abandoning the Hall of Orix and taking to the wilderness. All the people made haste and assembled on the great plain before the pallisades of the city, in the shadow of the Cyrian Highlands. The hosts of Manissa abided there for three days waiting for the word to go forth throughout her realm and for every man who could cast a spear to join her there. After three days, word was brought to her that Adaran had crossed the Erriad into Asylia and was laying waste the countryside round about him, and so she called Amyntas and said to him, "My lord Amyntas, most bold and trustworthy of all my counselors, it is you who breached the walls of Danath Hered and overthrew that mighty fortress, for which you have won my undying affection. I beg of thee one more boon, to which I will entrust to no other man." Amyntas knelt on the ground before her and said, "Whatever the queen commands I will do." She said, "Take three thousand horsemen and make a stand before the walls of Asylia. Engage Adaran, but not too hotly. As soon as you start to get encumbered, break off and give up the city, retreating to the west across the highlands to rejoin with me. Adaran must believe that he has routed us and thrown us into panic; he cannot know that we have willingly yielded our city to us. Thus must be our way with Adaran - yielding to him slowly, until the time to strike is at hand."

Amyntas said, "It shall be done, my lady." But Manissa was in great fear for him and grasped his arm, saying, "I tremble to give you this command, because in ordering it I am throwing you into the mouth of the lion and asking you to climb back out." Amyntas said, "The affection of my queen is reward enough," and went forth from her to assemble his riders. At the ninth hour of the that day, Manissa put off her gown and her delicate vestings and donned breeches and riding boots of leather, and buckled upon her legs greaves of gleaming bronze. Then she took from her hair the tresses, the intricate plaited braids and flowers that perpetually adorned it and instead had her maids fasten it in a single, tightly wound braid which hung down her back. Then she buckled her ' cuirass to her breast over her linen tunic and set greaves upon each arm, every piece polished and glimmering in the setting sun. She fastened about her the great green cloak which she had worn on her flight from Lissus to Cruachan and which she bore perpetually with her ever after. Finally she donned a helm of finely beaten brass, polished and rimmed with silver, made by the smiths of Kerion just for her, and leapt upon her great steed, mighty Ruah, whose coat was black as coal and whose feet caused the earth to tremble. Then Naross came to her and handed her the spear of Ioclus, that mighty beam which had felled many men and beasts, and Manissa raised it into the air and gave a mighty cry. Then all the peoples of Asylia struck camp and began moving westward, leaving behind only Amyntas and three thousand riders to engage Adaran.

But as Adaran passed through Asylia, there were many villages and towns which were unable to meet Manissa in time, or had not heard the summons, or otherwise did not come. These Adaran razed to the ground and put the inhabitants to the sword. Then he had the bodies flung upon the road and trampled under the feet of his army as it marched past. Two criers went before him with great horns, blowing them and announcing to the hills, "Thus shall be done to the people who opposes Belthazre, lord of the earth." But as many as were slain, the same number escaped and fled westward with what they could bring, hoping to come to Manissa in the Cyrian Highlands; some others fled south into the Badoan hills and others north into Ituria. All before Adaran the peoples were in rout, and the horizon was orange with the burning of villages. In the vicinity of many of the villages Adaran found a great number of finely bred Asylian steeds, some of which he had his men capture but many of which fled and ran wild into the wilderness between Asylia and the Erriad, and thus evermore have wild horses been found in that region, which the people call the *Marumar*, that is, Marudan Fire. All through that region Adaran burned and laid waste and slew all that crossed him, whether shepherd in the field or woman flying to the woods, all alike were put to death. Thus the land was desolate around him.

But when Adaran was but a day's march from the city of Asylia and the Hall of Orix, Amyntas mustered his men and said, "Now we ride to as tough a task as ever befit an Asylian rider: to leap into the mouth of the beast and back out again. Follow my orders and see that no man gets separated." Then the three thousand riders were formed up into three lines, one thousand each, and rode swiftly eastward behind Amyntas. What is sung of long-haired Amyntas of Kerion, who with the valiant three thousand rode out to face death at the spears of Adaran? At the head of the hosts of Asylia he flew in a fury, his locks blown behind his noble head, breast on fire for glory or death. His pressed his steed onward; sweat ran off the animal and glistened in the

96

burning summer sun, which parched the plains of Asylia and beat down upon Amyntas and his men. All alike followed behind their captain, horses' necks rearing, legs trampelling the brown earth, spears lowered and ready to strike deadly blows to the Marudans. After a time they came upon the host of Adaran, spread out over the plain like ants. Then long-haired Amyntas said, "Heed my words, you men of Asylia! We must fight hard enough to convince the Marudans that we intend to make our stand here, but not so hotly that we cannot withdraw when need be. Therefore we will make two assaults, and after this fall back upon Asylia and the hallowed beams of Orix's hall." Then Amyntas reared up like a lion ready to pounce, and roared a mighty roar, "Cruacha! Manissé e Cruachan!" and all the hosts of Asylia in their lines cried the same from the backs of their steeds. Amyntas held his mighty spear aloft, head gleaming in the heat of the day, and spurred his horse onward, the earth trembling beneath the hosts of Asylia.

Adaran was told that the Asylians were making a charge, and he ordered his chariots out to engage them on the plain, in whose company were Zimrah and Eluah, archers of great renown. The warriors leapt into their cars, the drivers lashed the reins and the brazen chariots of Caeylon sped forth upon the plains to halt the advance of Amyntas, wheeled chariot thrown against mounted rider upon the shrubs and grass of the Asylian plain. The hosts crashed into each other with great clanging and ringing of sword and spear upon shield. Many Marudans drew their bows and fired into the ranks of Amyntas, bringing down scores. But the Asylians maneuvered their horses more skillfully than did the charioteers their cars, and the lines of Amyntas circled about them and dealt death from all directions. But Zimrah said to his brother Eluah, "That long-haired fellow is the leader of them. Come, let us bring him down and the fight will be less hot." Eluah marveled at Amyntas and said, "See how he wheels this way and that, and everywhere he goes he leaves bodies in his wake! He looks more like a lion than a man! But I have shot both man and lion, and so will I bring down this arrogant barbarian." So Eluah and Zimrah drove their chariots into the place where Amyntas was leading his horsemen and fired upon him. But Amyntas dodged, and the arrows struck his horse and killed it from below, bringing him crashing into the dust beneath his fallen steed. Zimrah cried, "Amyntas is brought low! Fall upon him!" So all the charioteers closed in where Amyntas had fallen. But Amyntas threw his horse from him and stood erect, his hair disheveled and his teeth gnashed in rage, and he saw at a great distance Zimrah and Eluah directing the battle and firing their deadly arrows upon his men. Then he said, "These reckless sons of Maruda think they know what it means to cast death upon an enemy from afar? I shall show them how it is done!" Then he took his spear in hand, and picked up another from a slain Asylian. With one mighty beam in each hand caught the brothers in his deadly eye and made a great cast of the two shafts with all his strength. The spears whirred through the hot air and each hit their mark, Zimrah struck in the throat above the collarbone and Eluah in the heart, and both tumbled down from their chariots into the dust.

When the Caeylonics saw their captains slain, they panicked and withdrew, and Amyntas cried, "Form your lines!" and charged at the Marudans. The charioteers broke ranks and each went his own way, leaving the main body of Adaran's men open before Amyntas. The ranks of Asylia drew nigh to the Marudans, but they did not make the error of Eridax, for instead of dashing into them and becoming outflanked, they rode to within twenty yards and cast their spears, then rode off. Each spear hit its mark, mighty beams of cedar and ash crashing through bronze, dashing heads and tearing flesh. But Adaran brought forth Keniah, the greatest warrior of Caeylon, and said, "Break those Asylians upon thy shield!" Keniah therefore took a thousand men and formed a shield wall at the fore of the battle, so when Amyntas rode upon the Marudans the second time their blows of sword and spear were softened, for the shields of Keniah were strong. Then Amyntas cried out, "We can do no more here! Withdraw to Asylia!" Then the surviving horsemen turned their steeds to the west and sped forth towards the Hall of Orix, leaving many dead. They did not rest until they reached the pallisades of Asylia, and many men there collapsed from fatigue. But Amyntas harangued them and said, "Up! To arms! We must repeat our show again, this time making a spirited defense of this place before withdrawing, so that we may encourage them further west!" So the men took up positions within the pallisade, and it was found that seven hundred had fallen before Adaran on the plain.

When he saw that the horsemen had headed off, Adaran summoned Keniah and his advisor Bula and said, "They are clearly in rout. We must pursue them before they can fortify their capital. But this army is too great to move with much swiftness. Therefore

Keniah shall take three thousand of his swiftest men and march west to Asylia. Put it under siege with haste and encompass it about so there can be no escape, and I shall come aid you within two or three days at the most." So Keniah took up his great shield and mustered his men, as Adaran had commanded, and marched forth without delay towards Asylia. It took Keniah a day and a half to reach Asylia, for they marched by foot, though they stopped only briefly for rest. When they came upon the city, to their surprise, they found it much smaller than Cadarasia with defenses made of wood and earth rather than stone. Keniah laughed and said, "Shall wood and earth keep out Keniah, slayer of the Vecantian giants and first among all the warriors of Maruda?" Then he ordered his men to advance at once and throw firebrands into the city and torch the wooden pallisades. Amyntas said, "There is nothing we can do. We have neither enough men nor the food to withstand any siege, nor can we prevent them from firing our defenses. Therefore, let every man cast spear or stone at them and then mount your horses and flee westward until we come to the Cyrian Highlands and the folk of Asylia in flight."

So the Asylians all cast their spears, fired their bows and hurled stones and javelins at the Marudans, and while this did no great damage, it stopped them from getting too close to the pallisade. Then Amyntas and the Asylians mounted their steeds and made a sortie out of the city to the west, where Keniah had but a few sentries yet posted. Foolish Caeylonics! They attempted to stand between Amyntas and the west, bewteen the lord and his queen, and cast their spears as they may, the long-haired lord of Kerion rode them down, and the horsemen of Asylia trampled them into the dust. Thus Amyntas fled into the west.

But many of the Asylians were unable to remove themselves from the city, and the Caeylonics torched the walls and breached the pallisade. The fire frightened the horses and caused them to flee, and the trapped men said, "Our horses have fled. The end has come for us. Let us take refuge in the great hall of our forefather Orix, just as Garba perished in the Temple of Mironna." So the valiant among them, those who could fight and were not injured, fled to the Hall of Orix and bolted its door tightly. When Keniah took the city and came upon it, some of his advisors told him, "This is the great Hall of Orix, built by the seed of the union between Orianna and Manx. It was from here that Manissa and her father Ioclus reigned! Let it be spared!" But when Keniah found that the men hiding inside could not easily be ejected, he ordered the great hall set afire. Thus the Hall of Orix was torched, and the men inside perished in agony. The fire burned hot and quick and reduced wood and flesh alike to ashes, leaving only the two front posts intact, though charred and blackened. Thus was Asylia overthrown and the Hall of Orix burned to the ground.

Chapter 11
Asylia, Cyrenaica and Arcoria

While Amyntas was engaging Adaran upon the plains and Keniah was burning Asylia and the great Hall of Orix, Manissa and her people, together with all her lords, were fleeing westward. They ascended into the Cyrian Highlands and come several days journey into the west, to the borders of Asylia and the desolate places where the grass is short and the ground stony, and neither horses graze nor men abide. There upon the plain Manissa thrust her spear into the ground and called a halt to the march. She summoned her lords to her and said, "It will be several days before the Marudans reach Asylia and discern where we have gone, and how to pursue us. Our tracks are light over this stony ground. Therefore, let us pause to consider our course of action." So the Asylians struck camp and rested their weary bodies upon the dry earth. A census was made of all the people there with them, and it was found that nigh unto thirty seven thousand encamped on the plain with Manissa, including women and children.

Manissa summoned to her all her lords, some of whom had once counseled Ioclus. Among those at that council were Arrax, Naross of the Great Throw, Hadrior the cunning, Eridax, lord of Cadarasia and husband of Danica, and some of the lords of the Iturs. Manissa brought them into her tent and had her maidens seat them on fine furs and wait upon them. She herself was seated upon an ornate stool fashioned for her by the people of Paros, her uncle's kinsmen. While the men reclined upon the furs and drank, Manissa bore her thoughts to them: "Though our numbers are great, we are retarded in our progress by the women, children and elderly with us. If we are attacked by the Marudans, we will be found in great disorder and unable to defend ourselves from them upon this open plain. Therefore, I judge it best to send the women, children and the old away to the south, into the regions bordering Lugaria, where it is fertile and where they can find much shelter in the hills and among the villages of the Lugarians. They tread lightly and will leave no tracks upon this shallow, stony plain. Therefore, let them be sent away, that we may tighten our forces and prepare for the final encounter with the Marudans." Her lords agreed to this, and so the order was given that all women, children, elderly and anybody not fit to fight were to be sent away to the south, led and protected by only one thousand spearmen. They were ordered to be ready to depart within two days time. When they did depart and bid farewell to their men and their kinfolk with many tears and prayers, it was found that only a little less than ten-thousand remained, all of them hardened men of war experienced with the cruel spear and the sword.

Arrax rose and said, "My lady, you have said that we shall lead the Caeylonics westward until their supply lines run thin and they can no longer protect their rear, yet how can we make such a maneuver upon the desolate highlands, where there is neither rock nor tree for cover nor any hill or gorge to flee to if things go badly? Furthermore, what surprise can we hope to give them upon this plain?" Strong-armed Manissa replied, "You speak the truth, uncle, but it is not upon this plain that we will give the Caeylonics war, but in the wildernesses further west."

Hoary-headed Naross stood and said, "My queen, the wilds to the west of the highlands are not only unknown to the Marudans, but to our own men as well, for the Asylians have never ventured much further west than we have already come, for our eyes have ever been towards the east and the fair vales of Cadarasia, not westward into the desolate wildernesses. How shall we work any stratagem upon them if we know not the ground?" Manissa smiled upon her uncle and said, "Fate shall make an opening for us, but we must await word from our noble lord Amyntas of the engagement with Adaran and the fate of Asylia. Either way, west we must go, and I care not what we find when we venture there, only that we stay ahead of Adaran; only that we wear him down by constant pursuit, by the rigors of the march, by the fear that grapples men when they come into foreign and hostile lands, and finally by entrapping him in a distant place far from any friendly hearth, there to cut him down forever." Some of the lords protested, but stern Manissa would not relent, and it was decided that the flight westward would continue.

Then she called forth her brother-in-law Hadrior, he who had been married to Saraeth, and told him, "Go forth into the north, to Cyrenaica, and see if you can persuade the King of Cyrenaica to make an alliance with us now and strike the Marudans from the rear once they come westward upon the highlands." Hadrior was very put out by this, for he perceived that he was not to be part of the great campaign and battle, and thus would not win glory. But nevertheless he agreed and went forth at once to the land of Cyrenaica, many days ride north to the sea, where the sun ever shines. Then Manissa gave orders that riders be dispatched to the far southwest, to the westernmost marches of Lugaria, for the chiefs of the Lugars to come to meet with the Queen of Asylia at the western edge of the Cyrian Highlands three days hence. Then, seeing her lords were troubled, she soothed them and said, "I have been pursued and overtaken by the Marudans in the wilderness before, some years ago upon the slopes of the hills of Lissus, upon a woeful night fraught with rain and death for my house. They will pursue and will not relent, and in this we will undo them, for just as they surrounded and ambushed Ioclus and his sons within a wood in the dark hours of the night, so shall we entrap and destroy them and leave their bones to rot." Then the lords nodded in approval and cried out, "May it be as you say!" and feasted and talked into the night, reclining and drinking upon the soft furs of Manissa's tent, the vigilant warriors of Asylia encamped outside upon the hardened earth of the Cyrian plain beneath the pale and brilliant autumn stars. Thus it is sung in the tales.

But Adaran, after burning Asylia and destroying the Hall of Orix, lingered in the region for several days discerning what to do. His scouts returned to him and told him that the Asylian horsemen had ridden off to the west, into the highlands. But Bula came to him and said, "Master, the scouts report that the highlands are vast and desolate, covered only by short prairie grass and not much earth. They say it is rocky in many spots and that freshwater is scarce. It will not be able to support all our mighty hosts." Adaran said, "Neither would I want this rabble following us into battle, for they will only rob us of any chance of surprise and confuse our movements." Therefore many of the merchants, traders and settlers who had come in the train of Adaran decided to remain behind in Asylia. So Adaran issued a charter in the King's name and proclaimed all the lands hitherto ruled by Asylia from the Hall of Orix to be bestowed upon the people of Caeylon for perpetuity and encouraged the persons who remained behind to cultivate its fields, breed its horses and rebuild the city of Asylia to be the westernmost jewel of the Caeylonic empire. Then all the people cried out, "This we will do!" And as governor of the new territory he gave them none other than Arahaz, whom he called forth and invested with royal authority before all the people, and they all cried with one voice, "Hail, Governor Arahaz!"

But Arahaz spoke to Adaran privately, saying, "You mock me with this, Adaran." Adaran scoffed at him and said, "Rule your kingdom of ash, cripple! Thou outcast, rejected by gods and men and utterly cursed! Rule over the burnt buildings and the fallow fields, a king of rabble and prostitutes! I will deal with you when I return, and Belthazre will think none the worse of me for taking care of you for him." Arahaz said, "Let it be as you say: my death comes to me in this land, but it shall by no means precede your own." Then Adaran was filled with rage and struck Arahaz on the ear and knocked him to the ground, and the entourage of Adaran laughed greatly at Arahaz's pains and left him.

But Bula came and aided him and brought him into his tent to rest; and there ministered to Arahaz and brought him wine. Arahaz said, "I will not forget your kindness, yet I do not envy you, for the first time I pursued these people into the wilderness it came at the cost of my leg. I am not eager to make another like pursuit." Bula laughed and said, "Ever art thou the foreteller of evil and ruin! Here we feast and drink upon the ashes of their capital and yet you predict our own destruction!" But Arahaz said, "They are crafty and cunning, and I perceive that they allowed us to burn this place as a ruse only, and were the battle in earnest would have never delivered it up to us with so much ease." Bula said, "What looks like ease to you only shows forth the excellence of our own troops compared to yours." Arahaz said, "I shall take my leave now, for I have exhausted all I have in my heart. But before heaven I declare that I curse the day I ever heard the name of Asylia! Curses and evil upon that day, that bright and happy day, when my lord Belthazre who held me in high esteem summoned me to his chambers and asked me the name of the most beautiful maiden in Asylia, and I did tell him it was Osseia daughter of Ioclus, whose beauty has since vanished from the earth. Oh, that I had rather bitten my tongue off and spit it at his feet or perished by some accident before coming to his chambers, for I have become a pawn by the envy of the Queen Narússa, and now because of what I did to the Asylians upon the slopes of Lissus has all this woe come upon our land and have so many of our men perished upon these wildlands! Curse the day Anathar came to these lands, and ever cursed and thrice-condemned be the arrogance and foolishness of Belthazre and Narússa both, fitting mates and partners in stupidity!"

Bula said, "You go too far Arahaz, for though I look kindly

upon you and take it to my heart to aid you in your misfortune, I can do so openly no longer, for you have clearly spoken treason in my tent. Therefore take your walking-stick and go, and come unto me no more, for I will overlook your poisonous words this time, but should I hear such blasphemies come from you again I shall have you imprisoned and sent back to Caeylon as a traitor, where you will be put to the torment and slain." Arahaz only laughed and said, "Such is the end of all the servants of Belthazre, the worthy and the scoundrel. Nevertheless I will remember your kindness, and now I shall take my leave." Then Arahaz left the tent of Bula.

But Hadrior made his way northwards into the region of Cyrenaica, a journey across vast wildernesses of many days. Yet he was not entirely downcast, for when he arrived he expected to see Karyon, the servant of Eridax, who had escorted the emissaries of King Endumion of Cyrenaica back to their land not too many days past and had lingered there, for he had not returned. But when he came unto the region of Cyrenaica and felt the heat of the northern sun upon his face it came to pass that he was seized by a guard of Cyrenaicans in a vale not far the the city. They bound him with cords and treated him rudely, and when he protested that he was a kinsman of Manissa they only laughed and mistreated him more. They escorted him into the great city of Cyrenaica, called Thán, a glistening white city set upon the northern coasts of Elabaea like a ivory jewel, and brought him before the throne of King Endumion. Hadrior protested his treatment and asked to see Karyon and speak with him. But King Endumion told him how on the way back from the meeting with Manissa, the meeting at which Arrax had rashly suggested putting the ambassadors of Endumion to death, it came to pass that the Cyrenaicans betrayed Karyon and ambushed him, overtaking him in the night. They told Hadrior how they had brought him back to Thán bound as he himself was now bound and how they gave an account of the words and deeds of the Manissans before King Endumion. At this Endumion was very wrathful and said to Karyon, "So this is how your queen treats the servants of the King of Cyrenaica? If they do not at once assent to everything she says they are threatened with death and forbidden to set foot in her lands again? As the gods live, you shall die for this." Then he related how they took Karyon and cast him into a certain watery pit to be devoured by a monster they called Ochu, and therein he met his death. Hadrior was filled with grief and wept for Karyon, who alone among the men of Cadaras had

105

escaped the spears of Adaran when they had been encircled on the plains.

Then Endumion said, "So shall this one perish, for I will have nothing to do with Manissa or her wars." Then they seized Hadrior and led him into a courtyard of the king's palace where there was an open place surrounded by pillars and olive trees. In the midst of the yard was a great pit, greater than a man's height in its breadth, covered over with a large iron grate. The grate was removed by several eunuchs, and Hadrior was cast headlong into the pit, which was about twelve cubits in depth and full of water. At that time Ochu came forth from the depths, sensing that something had been cast into his water, and when Hadrior beheld the water bubbling and Ochu emerging beneath him he was filled with dread. Now this Ochu was a creature who had dwelt there since the ancient times, and when the city of Thán was built they enclosed the pit of Ochu, whose name means "pit rot" in Cyrenaican (for he is also called Ochuru, which means "pit mold"). The pit of Ochu sat in the midst of a great courtyard, for Ochu was bound to the water and could not emerge from the pit. His appearance was frightful, a series of protruding flaps overlapping, like large palm leaves laid one upon another, so that one could not tell whither was his head or whither was his mouth. His color was green, not the green of the grass but the green of sickness, and on the underside of the flaps were rows of small teeth, with which he was wont to tear and gouge his victims so as to weaken them with many wounds before dragging them down into himself to devour.

Hadrior raised himself up and struck at Ochu with his feet, keeping him at a distance. Meanwhile the eunuchs and servants of King Endumion gathered about the top of the pit, jeering and mocking Hadrior and making wagers on how long until the monster dragged him into the waters. But in those days Hadrior was full of strength and he would not let Ochu take hold of him, but instead he grasped the fleshy flaps of Ochu and with a great effort broke them off from his body. Then Ochu was furiously

106

Hadrior struggles with the creature Ochu as the servants of
Endumion look on in jest.

*Ochu came forth from the depths, sensing that something had been
cast into his water, and when Hadrior beheld the water bubbling and
Ochu emerging beneath him he was filled with dread...Meanwhile the
eunuchs and servants of King Endumion gathered about the top of the pit,
jeering and mocking Hadrior and making wagers on how long until the
monster dragged him into the waters.*

107

enraged and lurched his great hulk up to envelop Hadrior and took hold of him by the leg and would have pulled him under. But Hadrior clung to the wall of the pit, and so mightily did he grasp the wall that as Ochu pulled on him he pried forth a great stone from it, and once it was in his hand, he heaved it with all his strength against the hungry flaps of Ochu and crushed many of them. Then Ochu cried and bubbled and released the leg of Hadrior and sunk back into the pit in fright, and Hadrior was alone in the black water. Then the servants of Endumion and the eunuchs were greatly enraged and said, "He is greater than the other Asylian, whom Ochu devoured easily." So they threw down ropes and lifted Hadrior from the pit, intending to put him to death by some other cruelty.

But Hadrior was greatly enraged and a fury fell upon him, and when the eunuchs lifted him from the pit he seized the rope from their hands and formed a lash with it and struck them and drove them from the courtyard. But the servants of King Endumion he grasped and hurled into the pit, and Ochu came forth in a great rage due to the wound he had received and fell upon the servants, overtook them with his quivering flaps and pulled them down into himself. Thus they perished in the bubbling black froth. Hadrior would have run but he found that his leg was torn and mangled from the teeth of Ochu, and so he concealed himself in a bush until a servant of the king came thither on a horse to see what the furor was. Hadrior emerged from hiding and hurled the servant from the steed, and mounting upon it fled from Cyrenaica. But as he sped from the city he lifted his hand to heaven and swore a vow, saying, "By the beard of Manx and all the gods of the sky and earth, I shall be avenged upon Cyrenaica and Endumion for my leg and for the wickedness they have conceived against my queen. I shall return again to Cyrenaica and surely lay this city waste and put Endumion to death."

He made south for the Cyrian Highlands, but his leg grieved him sorely and he soon took ill with fever and could ride no more, for his mind was overtaken with blackness and he fell by the wayside. He lingered there for a day and a night in the throes of death until some shepherds found him. Perceiving him to be an Asylian of some importance, they took him west to a village called Baris, where they tended him and nourished him. When he came to and told how he had fought the beast Ochu, they thought him to be a god and called him *Achanor*, that is, "He who triumphs over the beast." The people of Baris treated Hadrior well, but he was sorely grieved because his leg was severely wounded and he was unable to ride or walk for many weeks. Thus he was unable to join Manissa or fight anymore against Adaran and did not come again to Asylia until the ending of the war, and ever after those days he walked with a limp. But he remembered the hostility of Endumion and brooded in his sickbed.

At that time Amyntas returned to Manissa with several of his men and reported that Adaran had been engaged and that the Hall of Orix was burned and Asylia overrun. So there was great wailing and lamentation all throughout the tents of the Asylians that evening, and Manissa made a vow that when she returned in triumph to the east that all her hair would be shorn off and burned in mourning for the Hall of Orix and the tombs of her fathers. Then she blew the trumpet and all the men of Asylia marshalled themselves for the march, striking camp and making their way westward over the Cyrian Highlands.

Now the Cyrian Highlands are rugged and stony, and the soil is shallow so that only short grasses and brambles can grow there. Manissa said, "We must make haste across this plateau, for if we should be overtaken and attacked there is nowhere to flee or take up a defense." So they pressed on westward across the highlands for two days, pausing only momentarly and taking their water from the few puddles and pools which sit upon the plain. The nights were clear and lighted by the moon and the stars, and they took their bearing by the sign of the Herdsman which shone over their heads in the starry firmament.

It is told of that journey how Manissa saw old Naross nodding upon his steed, and she roused him and said, "Awake uncle, for our fortunes are about to change in this affair!" He said to her, "My queen, I pray thee take no offense at the weak composure of one who has lived beyond his years, for I am part worn from this flight and part stricken with grief at the burning of Orix's great hall." But Manissa said, "No offense could you ever give to me, wisest of Asylians. Yet we must press on, for I feel a burning in my bosom that will not let me rest till we come to the wilderness which lies west of these highlands." Thus they spoke and rode throughout the evening.

After three days they came to the end of the highlands, where the land drapes down in great slopes and becomes a wilderness of beech and elm with an abundance of crabapple, fuil

109

of white blossom and sturdy holly clustered about the shadows of the greater trees. It was a fruitful and pleasant land, though one devoid of roads or any sign of habitation. It was into this region that Manissa came the third day after breaking camp. Thus the time of the Asylians upon the Cyrian Highlands was nine days from their departure from Asylia to their coming off of the highlands. Thus is the Feast of Novemor kept in those regions to this day recalling their flight.

As they struck camp in the western wilderness, it came to pass that the emissaries of the Lugars came to greet Queen Manissa, for they had harkened unto the words of the queen's servants and were waiting for the Asylians at the western slopes of the highlands, as Manissa had requested. The lords pitched their tents and rested their weary bones, and the men slumbered, but white-armed Manissa summoned the Lugarians and said to them, "Peace to you, fierce men of Lugaria. Ever has there been amity between our people and yours. What good word comes from thy king in Luxar?" The emissaries bowed to the queen, and said, "Great queen, your renown has reached even the pillared halls of Luxar where our lord in splendor reigns. We have heard the messengers which you sent to our nation and have come here to offer the words of our king, regal Karanus." Manissa said, "Let his words be heard."

Then the emissaries bowed and said, "King Karanus of the Lugarians says that the people of Lugar will aid the Asylians in all their exploits against the easterners, save only in the bearing of arms in combat. But if the queen desires us to serve as guides, or shelter her person or any other Asylian, or provide food and drink, any of these things will the Lugarians do faithfully. Already we shelter many of your womenfolk in our villages and will continue to do so till this matter be ended."

Manissa was pleased with this answer and said to the chief emissary, "What is your name, master Lugarian?" And he replied, "Alscetor, my lady." Manissa said, "Noble Alscetor, what is the name of this region wherein we are encamped? " And Alscetor said, "In our tongue it is called Arcoria my lady, though other peoples have diverse names for it." Manissa said to Alscetor, "It is a fair and pleasant land, full of lush grasses for the grazing of our horses and comely trees and flowering bushes to rest in. Why is it uninhabited?"

Then Alscetor said, "My lady, this land is uninhabited

because it sits in the shadow of the great wood." When Alscetor mentioned the great wood, fire was kindled in Manissa's bosom and she said, "I insist you speak of this wood." Alscetor said, "My lady, the Arcorian Wood sits heavy on this land, and its extent is great, so that no man dares to traverse it or even to abide in its shadow." Manissa said, "And what is so frightful about the wood?" Alscetor said, "Its furrows were plowed in the ancient days when the foundations of the mountains were laid, and its great boughs were sired by the Sons of Anak, the Mighty Ones of old, whose power has from thenceforth even unto this day rested upon the wood and made it a dread and a horror to men, for beside it all other forests are as clusters of weed upon the plain or rushes by the riverside."

Manissa said, "Is it then forbidden to enter the forest?" Alscetor said, "Nay, not forbidden my lady, but reckless." Then Manissa said, "By the beard of Manx, the Marudans have yet to see reckless! But it was my recklessness which led me to pursue my steed Ruah into the rain, so said my ill-starred brother Eleth. Also it was recklessness which led me on to continue my father's intention to wage war against the Caeylonics - and how have we fared? Have we not slain them from Asylia all the way to Danath Hered? Let them come and pursue us into this wood Arcorian, there to find bitter death at the point of our spears, and an end to their tyranny in the west once and for all." Then she sent Alscetor away with many gifts and bid him to do all he could to aid her in the conflict with Adaran, which he was eager to do.

Thus Manissa went forth to her men and stood upon a great stone and bid them rest, for they had made swift time across the plains and the pursuit of the Marudans was cumbersome due to their great numbers. Furthermore, she did not want to put too much distance between Adaran and herself, for she feared the Marudans would grow discouraged and turn back. Therefore they tarried in Arcoria and rested themselves for three days, feasting on the sumptuousness of that land. It is told in the tales of that time how Manissa found for herself a shaded grove beneath the boughs of a great beech and there reclined in the heat of the noontide to take her rest and be refreshed. Only at that hour did she remove her armor and don the flowing gowns of a lady of Asylia, and she often sent for maids to undo her great braid and let her hair fall loose.

There it was that as Manissa reclined in the shade one day,

dappled by the sun falling through the leaves, that Amyntas, lord of Kerion, came walking in the grasses and espied her and was struck with love for her by reason of her great beauty. Thus he approached her and they spoke together often beneath the beech tree, Manissa recalling the lament of Osseia beneath the terebinth of En Ganar in Enna and Amyntas recounting the heroic deeds he had accomplished in her service: the slaying of the captain Ungorah at the battle at Erriad, the overthrow of Danath Hered and the diversion of Adaran, and also the holding of Asylia and the flight across the Cyrian Highlands. And Manissa seemed pleasant and most beautiful to his eyes, like the beauty of Orianna as she sang beneath the cedars in days of old. Thus Amyntas idled his noons away with Manissa beneath the beech tree of Arcoria and softened her heart ever more towards him.

But after three days of rest, Manissa donned her helm, took the spear of Ioclus in hand and mounted Ruah, calling for a muster of all her men. When she had thus mustered them she found a little over six thousand men on foot and almost four thousand mounted. Then she bid each man to carry but a one week supply of rations on their back and bid the mounted men to send away their steeds, for they were to enter the tangled forest of Arcoria. The men carried out her command with great trembling, for there were many legends about the great wood that affrighted them and made them uneasy. But the presence of the queen steeled their hearts against fear. Then Queen Manissa summoned Alscetor and said, "Behold, despite thy warnings it is my intent to lead our people into the Arcorian Wood, into whence we shall draw Adaran and from within where we shall strike him with such fury that Belthazre shall feel the very foundations of his throne shaken, though he be as far away as the sunrise." Alscetor said, "The queen is fearless and bold. What would you have us to do?"

Manissa said, "Abide here until the coming of Adaran, but feign that you are simple Lugarian tribesmen, not emissaries of the great King Karanus. Shed your royal garments and don simple skins, and tarry until the coming of the Marudans. Then they shall say to you, 'Where did the Asylians go?' and you shall tell them that not more than a few days prior you saw us enter the great wood, starving and frightened, and that we had let our horses go because we had no more feed for them. Then Adaran will be puffed up with arrogance and pursue us." Alscetor said, "I swear by the gods of Lugaria and the name of my good King Karanus that it

112

shall be done as you have requested." Then Alscetor and the Lugarians put off their garments and took on the apparel of simple huntsmen. But the Asylians formed up in good order and marched west, down the easily sloping meadows of Arcoria until they came unto the great shadow of the wood and the lurking green darkness that stretched across the horizon as far as the men could see. Arrax said to Manissa, "The very sight of it fills me with foreboding," but Manissa said, "Yet it shall turn to our glory." Thus they progressed across the bracken of the moorlands all that day until they came to rest at moonrise by the trunks of the great wood.

Chapter 12
The Pride of Adaran

Manissa summoned Naross her uncle and said, "I have great fear for Hadrior my brother, for he not yet returned to us nor sent word from Cyrenaica, though he ought to have been back several days ago." Naross said, "Something is amiss in Cyrenaica, for neither have we heard from Karyon, companion of Eridax, who was sent thither before we left Asylia to escort the emissaries of Endumion homeward. I suspect some treachery on the part of the Cyrenaicans and fear that we shall have no rear attack on Adaran when he arrives." Manissa was greatly troubled, but Arrax said, "No matter. We have come thus far and cannot remove ourselves now, for the enitre army of Maruda is between us and our homes. Let us press on into this wood as our lady has said and we will deal with the Marudans in our own way without recourse to Cyrenaican aid." So Manissa agreed to this counsel and gave the order to set forth into the woods of Arcoria.

Now the Arcorian woods are very great, so that the Lugarians say that there is no greater wood any place in the world, and its origins are full of legend. Nevertheless, it is only gradually that one comes into the depths of the wood, so that going west from the foot of the highlands one first ascends several miles of gently sloping country full of poplar, birch and evergreen, where the grasses are tall and the deer are plentiful. But by and by the trees become more dense and the field grass gives way to shorter grasses and finally to moss as one comes to the easternmost marches of the forest itself, where great oaks, beeches and elms grow so large that two men cannot easily reach their arms around their trunks, and where the light of the sun comes through only in dappled spotlets. Further in one comes to the most ancient region of the wood, where the broadleaf trees fall away before great pines of remote antiquity that tower upward into a dark canopy that sun cannot penetrate, draping the forest in a thick shadow and rendering the day like dusk. It is said among the people of Lugaria that were one to traverse the forest from east to west it would take at least a fortnight, but not all agree upon this, for some say that the forest is the very ending of the world.

Thus it was that Manissa led the hosts of Asylia westward into the forestland, and after two days of traversing the light woods came into the regions where the sunlight begins to fail and the great wood begins, and the men followed her on foot. Only Manissa and her lords retained their steeds, Manissa upon black Ruah going before the men draped in her green cloak, her armor glistening in the sun beams that fell through the forest canopy. They stopped only a few times for rest and continued the march throughout the nights until they were deep in the tangled wood and had to move slower, for there was no trail and each man had to make his own way as best he could. At the eve of the third day in the wood Manissa led them into a great clearing wherein there were a number of great trees that had fallen. Then she said, "Let us set up our camp here and discern what is to be done next, and from here to reconnoiter the land and deduce from where exactly we shall strike the Marudans." So the weary Asylians struck their camp in the clearing, but many slept on the ground or in makeshift huts, for a great number of them had left their gear behind to lighten their load when they released their horses.

Manissa was wearied from the rigors of the travel and decided against any action that evening, for all the men were hungry and tired. Therefore she retired to her tent to take her rest, but before retiring said to her lords, "Let Eridax be in charge of the first watch, Naross the second and Amyntas the third. See to it that the camp is secure and that the men put out their fires before darkness falls, for in this dark wood who knows what the flames of our watchfires may attract?" Thus she retired for the evening, and after removing her armor and donning her sleeping gown, laid upon some animal skins to take her sleep. Yet she was tormented and could find no rest, for her spirit was troubled by a great restlessness and there was unease in her mind. Shortly after midnight, a sentry came to her tent and said, "Arouse thyself my queen, for the lord Naross requests thy presence at the outskirt of the camp." So Manissa leapt up and donned her breeches and her green cloak and went forth into the night following the sentry. All about her the men of Asylia slept huddled upon the ground about smoldering coals, and the moon was full in the sky casting pale light over everything she beheld.

She was led to the edge of the camp where hoary-headed Naross stood crouched behind a fallen trunk, staring into the night. She approached him warmly and said, "What does your eagle eye perceive, uncle?" But he quieted her and bid her sit with him behind the great trunk, and when she did so he dismissed the other

115

sentries who were standing guard with him, so that he and Manissa were left alone in the moonlight behind the trunk. She was greatly distressed by this and said, "Uncle, tell me plainly, what so catches your eye that you awake me from my sleep and consider so weighty that you send away all your sentries when I come unto you?"

But Naross continued gazing into the night and said to Manissa, "Look out yonder, into the woods about fifty paces from the edge of camp, where the trees form a small open grove around that mass of rock." Manissa stared for a moment but saw only the great stone illumined in the moonlight - but after a moment her eyes fell upon a wondrous sight. Behold! Upon the rock within the grove leapt a great stag, akin to the one she had seen when, fleeing from Lissus, she collapsed in the wilderness by the spring. The stag was great and splendorous, shining white in the light of the full moon striking it in the grove, almost glowing, and bathing the surrounding trees in a strange silver cast. Manissa's breath left her, and she panted with longing and said to her uncle, "Uncle, I do believe I have seen this very stag before! When I fled from Lissus and was lost in the wilderness on the way to Cruachan, I saw this creature before me at a spring in the heat of the midday. Ever since I have longed to gaze upon it once more, and though I thought it could never be, my heart told me that I would again have this creature in my sight, though I knew not when! Now that I see him, and in the moonlight upon this rock, the stag is more glorious and beautiful than even I remembered."

But Naross said, "Tis no stag, my lady! Do you not recognize a Lamassu when it is before you? In the days of old (at least so it is told among the Lugarians and remembered by some old men of Asylia), the great Agenor came unto this land seeking a place to keep his great herds. Now Agenor was one of the Anakim, the Sons of Anak, Mighty Ones of old, who in our tongue were called *titani*. Thus it is told how Agenor came westward and ploughed the furrows of this forest himself and laid the seeds from which sprung these great trees. Then, when the wood was fully grown, he made it a home for his herds, the Lamassu. For many generations of men Agenor dwelt here, shepherding his herds of stag and doe

The Sacred Stag of Agenor, the Lamassu

Behold! Upon the rock within the grove leapt a great stag, akin to the one she had seen when fleeing from Lissus...The stag was great and splendorous, shining white in the light of the full moon striking it in the grove, almost glowing, and bathing the surrounding trees in a strange silver cast.

and leading them where he would.But then came the days when the Sons of Anak removed themselves from the world, and the forest of Agenor became overgrown and tangled, and his herds wandered aimlessly where they would. Most all of the stags of Agenor have since perished, but some have endured, rare though they are. This undoubtedly is one of the Lamassu, which are of such few number that a man may live seven lifetimes and never see one."

Manissa wept, "Then what does this portent for me, who hath laid my eyes upon this hallowed creature two times in almost as many years?" Naross said, "It is told among the elders that the sighting of a Lamassu portents great blessings and fortune for the one who sees it, though it also brings with it a great sadness." Manissa said, "This I bear witness to, for since the day I first set eyes upon the creature my heart has pined away with melancholy to behold it. Yet if thy words be true, then this must portent a glorious victory for the hosts of Asylia and a ruinous defeat for the Marudans! For it appeared to me as I was about to ascend to the chair of Ioclus, and now it again appears at a crossroads, when we must soon engage the fierce easterners for freedom or death in these woods of gloom."

Then she said, "This conversation is sweet, uncle, but now I will leave thee and go out to this creature, for I have so desired to go to it this long time." But her uncle restrained her and said, "Such a thing is not permitted, nor has it ever been told in the tales of Asylia, Epidymia or Lugaria that it has ever been done. Nay, remain here and adore from afar." But as Naross spoke the stag reared its mighty head and bounded off the rock into the dark wilds. Manissa leapt and would have pursued it, but Naross restrained her. Then she returned to her tent and wept until she fell into a bitter sleep.

The following morning the queen rose early and called upon Arrax, asking him, "Uncle, how do you heal?" He said, "Well, my lady, for the wound is but a light one and nothing to prevent me from drawing swords against the Marudans." She smiled and said, "This shall you do sooner than you think." Then Manissa gave word that scouts should be sent into the surrounding woods to survey if there were any paths and report on the layout of the land and the best strategy to entrap the Marudans. Thus Manissa and her lords waited and pondered what to do, but Manissa earnestly desired the stag and would have mounted Ruah and went forth searching for him had pressing matters not detained her in the camp.

Adaran meanwhile passed over the Cyrian Highlands, though much slower than the Asylians had by reason of the size of his army. Everywhere he passed he left desolate, for the marching of the hosts of Caeylon destoyed the grass and left the highlands a place of sedge bush and dust, as it remains to this day. After more than a fortnight he brought his army to halt at the foot of the highlands on the west bordering Arcoria, near the region where Manissa had come some time earlier. There he marshalled his troops and found he had twenty four thousand men who drew the sword. It was also there, as determined by Manissa, that he encountered Alscetor and the Lugarians tarrying in the land arrayed in the clothes of simple shepherds. Adaran had them seized and dragged before his chair and said, "Tell me, from whence do you come?" Alscetor and his companions said, "We are shepherds of Lugaria, my lord. We have wandered under the summer stars to seek the pasturelands of fair Arcoria, which you see about you, upon which we ever graze our flocks." Bula scoffed and said, "Then why have you no flocks? Do you presume to deceive us so easily?"

Then Alscetor feigned a great rage and said to Bula and Adaran, "Not four days a great host of barbarians passed this way going west into the great wood of Arcoria. They treated us roughly and took from us our flocks without any payment. They said they were fleeing from the men of Caeylon and needed our flocks for sustenance, as they had traveled far and were sorely tired and hungry." Then Adaran rejoiced and said, "Do you hear this, Bula? We have pursued them to the point of despair and are but four days behind them! But tell me herdsmen, said they anything about where they were destined?"

Alscetor said, "They said they meant to cross the Arcorian woods and settle on its westernmost reaches in the pleasant grasslands there. But many were against this and proposed to surrender themselves to you, though their queen dissuaded them." Adaran rejoiced to hear the false report of Alscetor and said, "Unity is broken within their ranks! We shall overtake them with ease. Herdsman, how great is this forest and how best can an army move through it?" Alscetor said, "I have never traversed it, my lord, but I think it to be no greater than a three day journey across, or so my people say." This he spoke deceptively, for in truth it would have taken a fortnight. Then Alscetor said, "If my lord desires to pursue

119

them they cannot have gone far, for their horses were weak and sickly, and many were abandoned for lack of feed. Had they had more time, perhaps they could have grazed them here, but they were in a sore hurry and abandoned their steeds, fleeing into the wood on foot, as men in their last desperation." Then Bula said, "If this be true, then they cannot be but a few days ahead of us. We can easily overtake them within the wood, since we are rested and they are destroyed from weakness and hunger."

Adaran became puffed up with pride and said, "You bring me good tidings, master shepherd. Name your price for this good word and it shall be given to you." Alscetor said, "Only bring back the head of that pretender queen who robbed me of my flocks and it shall be enough!" Adaran was deceived by Alscetor's words and believed him, and ordered Bula to give him a sack of silver to compensate him for his lost flocks.

Then he dismissed Alscetor and the Lugars, who wandered south and hid themselves in the wildlands there. But Adaran rested his men and prepared to enter the wood, and shortly thereafter gave the command for the hosts of Caeylon to marshall and enter the wood in pursuit of Manissa. At the head of the front column he placed Omer the Fast, who was hot for the blood of Arrax in vengeance for his kinsman Tegleth whom Arrax slew. Keniah the Caeylonite was given command over the bulk of troops in the center, and behind him Adaran with Bula his advisor. The Kushites were placed in the rear, and their champions Anurah, Olrath and Negurac were set in command over them, and this because the Kushites greatly feared and mistrusted the great wood, the likes of which they had never seen in their own land, and could not be compelled by any threat to enter first, for they thought the wood to be a haunt for evil spirits.

But when the Marudans entered the wood, the brush was too dense for them to move with any ease and the army of Adaran became greatly stretched out and thinned, so that it took a full day's march to go from the front to the rear. Then Bula came to Adaran and said, "My lord, the length of our column leaves me ill at ease. We have no way of knowing what goes on at the head or the rear for we are too thinned out. Furthermore, we have been now several weeks in this wilderness west of Asylia and are wanting in provisions. Our nearest fortress is at Asylia, which is almost a fortnight to the east across the arid plains and is ill secured at that, for its walls are still torn down and it is in the care of Arahaz, the cripple. What if the barbarians should double back behind us and strike Arahaz so as to cut us off without supply in this desolate place?"

Adaran was ill pleased by his words and said, "What do thou propose?" Bula said, "Let us return to the foot of the highlands and establish a fortress to winter there so as to strengthen ourselves in this land and to reinforce Asylia. Then let us pursue and smite the followers of Manissa in the spring." But Adaran scoffed and laughed saying, "You talk like a female, or less than a female; like Arahaz himself! Did you not hear the report of the shepherds? The Asylians are greatly stressed and near destruction. Far be it from me to have it told to Belthazre that I pursued Manissa this far, to the very ends of the world, only to let her escape. Nay, we shall pursue until we have encircled and destroyed her. Then when I return, I shall put my foot on the neck of Arahaz and slay him for his arrogance." Thus Adaran spoke many boastful things.

Meanwhile the scouts of Manissa returned and told her, "The Marudans enter the wood from due east, four days march from here, but they move with reluctance and many of their hosts are timid and fearful of the breadth of this great wood." Then Manissa said to her lords, "Let one of you go forth and pester the Marudans from a distance, that we may taunt them and cause Adaran to feel the pride of victory within his grasp and venture a little further into the wood." Then Eridax said, "I will go, my lady." And even as Adaran was speaking with Bula, Eridax gathered a host of one thousand picked men and bid them leave off all their armor and baggage and take only two javelins each. Then swift-footed Eridax led them by the deer-trails back eastward, pausing only momentarily to catch their breath or drink from a spring, until in two days time they encountered the forward force of Omer the Fast leading the Caeylonic column through the woods. Then Eridax shouted, "For Manissa and the Hall of Orix!" and came upon the column suddenly from the southwest, emerging from the tangled wood and hurling his javelins at the Marudans. His yell was fierce and his throws sure, and each javelin slew a man.

Then the rest of the Asylians rushed upon Omer's column from the darkened trees, each man casting their javelins, and upon casting, fled back into the wood. But Eridax was pursued by Omer, for he had not reckoned on Omer's great speed. Omer took Eridax by the cloak and would have slain him, but Eridax cast off his cloak and fled. Then Omer took account of his warriors and found three hundred had fallen slain before Eridax, but not one of the Asylians perished. When this was told to Adaran, he was filled with fury and swore by Adar and Mardu to never rest nor turn back until he had taken his vengeance on the Asylians. Then all his officers and men said, "Yea, even so." So Adaran's grand army of Maruda marched further and further west into the thickness of the Arcorian.

But Eridax returned to Manissa and cried, "It is as you said, my queen. They pursue us hotly and think to overtake and destroy us! Let us lay our snare for them now while their blood is hot and they will surely fall into it!" Manissa was greatly pleased by this report and went to consult bold Arrax, saying to him, "Uncle, arise, for before three days pass thy sword shall drink blood. Tell me, are you certain your wound has healed?" Fearless Arrax stood before her, strong and mighty and clutched his death-bringing spear, saying, "My queen and my kinswoman, I am resolved to follow you into battle whensoever you shall call me and not turn back until I have drenched my hands in gore." Then Manissa said, "You of all Asylians are the most powerful, the greatest of the sons of Ancyrus in might and the most favored chief of my father, Ioclus. Therefore, you shall lead the attack against Adaran when I shall command it." Arrax rejoiced and grasped the hem of Manissa's robe, and kissing it, said, "This day you have given me great glory in Asylia by entrusting this task to me, for it shall be sung of unto the ending of the world how Arrax son of Ancyrus pursued and slew Adaran. My name shall be great among the nations. But woe to Adaran, woe to that whelp of a lion! For this very day by entrusting the attack to me you have doomed him to death." But Manissa said, "Yet fate will have all things as she orders." Then Manissa ordered her people to marshall themselves according to their companies and prepare for war, for the day of reckoning upon the arrogance of the Marudans and in vengeance for the blood of lordly Ioclus, noble Garba and innocent Osseia. So the Asylians roused themselves to combat, and Manissa said, "Let us abandon this clearing and move further west, but leave what can be spared, for we must cause the Caeylonics to believe we left in great haste and fear." So the Asylians heeded the words of Manissa and abandoned the camp, moving westward into the densest part of the Arcorian woods.

But as Adaran's column proceeded into the wood, the trees became denser and the paths more difficult to travel for such a great force. His lines were stretched back even further, so that it would have taken one or even two days to go from the front to the rearguard. Furthermore, Omer's company, which was in front, thought to make pursuit of Eridax and went at a faster pace than Adaran's, and thus they soon came far out in front of the main body of men and did not keep due west but straggled in a southwesterly direction. By nightfall scouts reported to Adaran that they had lost contact with Omer. Futhermore, the Kushites in the rear were lagging further behind, for they were in great fear of the wood and of ambush, even more so since word got to them of the assualt of Eridax. Adaran seethed with fury and said to Bula, "Old Arahaz warned that we would perish at the hands of the Asylians, but I see my army is bound to defeat me by their own foolishness before we ever catch glimpse of one Asylian spearhead!" And he levelled many fearsome curses on his men as they moved beneath the shaded bowers of the Arcorian Wood.

By and by they came upon the clearing in which the Asylians had been encamped, and according to the will of Manissa, found many of the Asylians tents and belongings left behind, as though the Asylians had retreated in great haste. Then Adaran was exultant and said, "See, they fly in fear of us! Therefore let us fortify this position and from it sortie out westward to exterminate these barbarians." Then he took counsel with Bula and determined to camp in the clearing until the legion of Omer the Fast could be found, and to give time for the Kushites to catch up, for they were more than a full day behind. Thus the Marudans camped in the clearing, but so great was their number that only the few companies under Adaran could make room to pitch their tents within it. The remainder of the men had to dwell in the forest, and because their number was so great each man spread out where he would and pitched his tent as best as he was able. There was great confusion in the camp, for by reason of the dense wood they could set up with very little order and failed to post any picket or night watch throughout the camp. But each man clustered with others and built small fires, so that every man was a watch unto himself. Only Adaran set a watch around the main clearing, lest he be surprised by another Asylian ambuscade. Thus dusk came, the sun set, and darkness came upon the Arcorian Wood.

As dusk settled, Manissa's scouts said to her, "The Marudans are encamped in the clearing and in the woods surrounding it, and they are in great disarray." Then Manissa blessed the stag, the

Lamassu of Agenor and said, "Good fortune indeed! The enemy has been delivered into our hands this very night, and how fortuitous it is, for our provisions are nearly out." Then she summoned the lords of the Asylians and all the foremost captains and said that the attack would be made that evening, while the Marudans were weary from much marching, had lost word of their advance force and had no formidable picket or defenses but their great numbers. And all the lords were hot with bloodlust and clashed their spears and shields, crying, "Let it be so!"

When darkness fell, around the first watch, Manissa mounted Ruah (for she alone was mounted) and led her warriors eastward half a league to the outskirts of the Caeylonic camp. Every man was armed with heavy spear and brazen sword whetted for death and bore sturdy shields of oak overlaid with strips of hide. They advanced not in a column, but in elongated ranks so that the camp could be somewhat encircled and struck from sundry directions at once.

As they approached the encampment of the Marudans, they saw scores of fires burning before them in the darkness with the shadows of men around them, and some of the Asylians were affrighted and said, "This is their nightwatch! Surely we cannot hope to surprise them now!" But Manissa advanced further towards the fires, and perceived that they were not watchfires but only bonfires and that there was no picket line but only small groups of soldiers encamped together. Then her heart leapt within her and she said, "We have wandered right up to the Marudan camp! To arms! Do what you must but maintain stealth as long as is prudent." Then she led a dozen soldiers to one of the camp fires, around which seven men were resting and reclining. She grasped the great spear of Ioclus in her hand and neither cried out the battle call of the Asylians nor spoke any rousing words to her troops, but quickly and silently emerged from the darkness before the fire and hurled the spear at the nearest man, a Lysonian named Erath, not yet a man of twenty and still much a boy. He was reclining against a great pine when the fury of Manissa singled him out and took his life from him. The throw was sure and the blade sharp; the spear crashed through his ribs and stuck him there to the tree, his life blood spilling out in bubbling gasps. The men about the fire leapt up, but the Asylians came forth from the darkened wood and slew them quickly, so that no one had time to raise the hue and cry.

Thus Manissa led her band from fire to fire in the wood, and

124

thus did the other lords do so, wringing death around the outlying encampments. In many they found the Marudans resting in their tents, and death came easily to such as they found. They laid themselves down, prayed to their gods, and closed their eyes in peace, thinking to awake to the cool of the morning. But they never awoke, for they were slain on their pillows. But shortly before midnight they came deeper into the camp of the Caeylonics, where the fires were closer together and nothing further could be gained by stealth. Then Manissa, mounted upon Ruah clutching the gore covered spear of Ioclus, reared her steed in the orange light of a Marudan fire and cried, "Cruacha!" Then she burst forth into the midst of one of the camps, striking any Marudans who were ill-fated enough to find themselves within reach of her battle hardened spear arm. Then the Asylians rushed upon the camp from various places, some crying, "Cruacha!" and those from Cadarasia shouting, "Cru Cadara!" and other peoples each shouting their own diverse battle calls, so that he night air was filled with the frightful shouting of the hordes of Manissa.

The men of Caeylon leapt to their feet and aroused themselves from slumber, shaking the sleep from their eyes and banding together to make some defense, but to little avail, for the Asylians were upon them from every quarter. If they formed together to strike left they were assaulted from the right, and if they looked right they were besieged from the left, and many Marudans fell by their fires before they could take up arms or strike at the Asylians. It is said that in that first attack Andarat the Caeylonic war-captain was slain by Manissa, for he came forth from his tent heeding the cries of his troops and came upon the green-clad maiden, mighty and terrible atop Ruah dealing out death with her father's spear. This Andarat thought to take Manissa down and win the praise of Belthazre, and so cast forth his spear at her, but it crumpled uselessly against the great shield of Ioclus, four layers of hide overlayed with beaten bronze and rimmed with delicate silver ornaments. She turned on him like a lioness deprived of her cubs, and the fury of Manx was in her eyes. He turned to flee, but she caught him in her eye and cast her spear - a deadly throw! It struck him squarely in the back and felled him, his face crashing to the dust.

But Nabuzar and Polassur, renowned warriors of Caeylon, perceived the clamor in the outer camps and sent Zeleth, another captain, to run to Adaran and tell him of the ambush. So Zeleth went forth to find Adaran, but Nabuzar and Polassur gathered to them each a thousand men and went forth to the west side of the camp, where the din or war was the loudest. This was where Amyntas and Eridax were bringing the fight to the Marudans, making a great slaughter among them. Then Nabuzar said to Polassur, "You shall engage the youth, and I the long-haired captain. Whichever of us prevails first shall come to the aid of the other." So Polassur brought his spearmen through the underbrush to the place where Eridax was leading the Asylians in wreaking havoc among the Marudans. Polassur cast his spear, striking Eloss, a kinsman of Danica, the wife of Eridax. Also slain by Polassur were Aîonth, Talus and Dæclus, all stout men of Asylia who had been with Manissa since the battle with Tegleth at the Erriad.

The spearmen of Polassur came forth shoulder to shoulder, a wall of shields, and pressed the Asylians and would have driven them back, had not Eridax roused them and said, "Do not fear this hot-headed Marudan! I shall rid us of him." Then Eridax wrenched the spear from the body of Eloss his kinsman, a fine Caeylonic beam of Lysonian cedar, and hurled it at Polassur. The blade pierced him above the collar bone and tore his throat, so that he fell to the earth as his life drained from his open neck. Then the Marudans panicked and broke ranks, and Eridax said, "Fall upon them! The battle is ours!" So the Asylians roared with fury and said, "Cruacha! Manissé e Cruachan!" and pursued the Marudans, striking a great number of them with the edge of the sword as they fled.

But Nabuzar had engaged Amyntas some distance from where Eridax fought. Nabuzar struck the shield of Amyntas with his blade, pounding the beaten bronze in hopes of shattering it and slaying lordly Amyntas. But long-haired Amyntas dug his feet into the earth and threw back the assaults of Nabuzar, and raising his sword aloft, struck Nabuzar between the shoulder and the neck and hewed him down the middle, so that one half of Nabuzar fell one way and another the other way, for Amyntas did cleave him in two. Thus perished Nabuzar. And all the men of Nabuzar who saw this became faint-hearted, and their knees became as water. But Amyntas roared like a bear and cast his deadly spear, striking Danorah (the shield-bearer of Nabuzar) in the gut and piercing him so that the spear tip came forth from his back. He cried out with a loud voice and died, and likewise all the men under Nabuzar were put to rout or slain by the campfires.

Meanwhile Zeleth came unto Adaran and told him of what was going on outside the camp. Then Keniah begged to be given leave to go out and make war upon them. But Adaran, who was reclining at meal, said, "This is but a ruse! Starving and weakened as they are, would they dare attack the main camp of the army of Caeylon in the night? Nay, for they hope to weary us and deny us sleep, for they know tomorrow we shall march forth and annihilate them. They wish only to draw off our forces into endless hunts in the dark amidst these accursed trees. Let Zeleth return and take command of the outer defenses, and bother me not again unless the fighting becomes any hotter. I give thee command Zeleth." But Keniah pressed Adaran and pleaded to be sent forth, and Adaran became angered and said, "It is of no consequence what Zeleth tells us, for it is but a trifle and nothing that cannot be put down by such captains as we have." So Keniah kept silent, though his heart bid him ill tidings.

Thus Zeleth returned to the outer camps with the words of Adaran in mind, full of pride about the great deeds he would do and the name he would make for himself by slaying the Asylians. When he came forth to the camps, he did not perceive that both Polassur and Nabuzar had been slain and their forces routed. Therefore, he saw the shadows of the Asylians about the firelight and took them to be his own countrymen. He walked cheerfully up to the Asylians, proud of his own command that had been entrusted to him by Adaran, and greeted them, saying, "Praised be Mardu, for Adaran has entrusted the chastisement of the Asylian troublemakers to me!" But as he came into the firelight he saw not his countrymen but only merciless Arrax in the yellow glow, gore-covered spear in hand and grim scowl on his face, surrounded by hardened Asylian men of war. Arrax said, "Praised be Mardu indeed who has delivered you into my hands!" Zeleth pleaded on his knees with Arrax for his life, but cruel Arrax struck him with his sword and sent his head tumbling into the dust. Thus ended the brief and uneventful command of Zeleth.

The battle raged hotly around the outer camps of the Marudans, Manissa attacking from the southwest, Arrax, Amyntas and Eridax pressing hard from the west and old Naross attempting to circle beyond the encampments and strike them from the northeast. By midnight the Caeylonics were under siege from various positions, and a general cry was raised in the extremities of the camp. Word was brought to Adaran shortly after midnight, who was resting on a pile of furs in his tent, that there was a general melee at the edges of the camp, though as of yet the Asylians had not assaulted the main forces of Adaran within the clearing, nor even advanced within sight of it, but were slaying all who had dwelt outside the clearing under the trees within the wood. Therefore Adaran was greatly enraged at Zeleth and called for Keniah, saying to him, "Rally your men and go forth to the westernmost reaches of our position and secure it." So Keniah went away rejoicing, for he greatly desired to meet the Asylians in battle, especially Arrax whose fame was even known among the Marudans.

Then Adaran sent for Anurah, a captain of the Kushites, and said, "Send your fastest runners eastward along the forest road and find the Kushite troops who lag behind there. Tell them we are under attack and command them to double their speed to come to our aid." So Anurah sent forth a runner, Ribah by name, to find the Kushites who were lagging behind. It was not until the darkest hours of the night that Ribah came upon the Kushites, encamped upon the road little more than half a league east. But when he brought the message to their captains, they reasoned among themselves and said, "It is as we feared; the barbarians have lured us into this forest to slay us in the night. Come and let us leave Adaran to his fate." Their lords, Olrath and Negurac, protested and recalled to mind the oaths of fealty they had sworn to Adaran to serve him. Thus a great debate arose among the Kushites, and the captains all took up arms and overcame Olrath and Negurac and slew them. Upon seeing Olrath and Negurac dead, they were thrown into a great fear of what Adaran would do to them and said, "Let us slay the messenger as well so no word of this reaches him till we have fled east." So they seized Ribah and struck off his

128

head. Then the Kushites broke camp and fled east away from the battle, some three thousand men in all.

But Keniah gathered several thousand of his warriors and passed through the picket at the outskirts of the clearing, making his way west into the darkened woods towards where the cries of battle were the fiercest. As he led his men through the underbrush, he encountered many Marudans in flight from the outer limits of the camp towards the clearing where Adaran dwelt. Some of these he slew as cowards, but others he commanded to be seized and made to join his ranks, for there was great terror in the outer camps at Arrax and the other lords who were raging about in the darkness or by firelight and striking all whom they met. After some time Keniah saw fires in the distance and heard loudly the din of arms crashing and the cries of war. Then he told his men, "Form up in a line and let no Asylians pass by." So his men formed a great line, a thousand or more strong, and levelled their flesh-shredding spears. At their head stood Keniah, fierce and bold, bearing the great shield overlaid with four layers of hide which he had taken from a Vecantian giant he had slain. Then he saw in the shadows and amidst the glow of the fires the figure of Arrax, sword in hand, moving to and fro bringing death to all about him and said, "This can be none other than Arrax, brother of Ioclus and slayer of Tegleth. Let us press the Asylians back, but I decree that no man great or small should make war on Arrax save myself, for I would see if his might is equal to what is spoken of him." Thus Keniah advanced, his sword thirsty for the blood of raging Arrax.

Yet Arrax knew not of the approach of Keniah, for until then they had met little resistance among the Marudans and did not know whether their assault was known of by Adaran or not. Furthermore, the darkness of the night and the stealth of Keniah's approach deceived Arrax, and the Marudans were upon him before he was aware of them. Keniah's warriors charged the Asylians and thrust with their spears, piercing many through and driving them back. Arrax tried to rally them, but the Marudans cast their spears and slew a great many of Arrax's host, so that the Asylians were hard pressed to keep up the fight, and many of the men bid Arrax to retire from the battle. But Arrax said, "This Marudan is no bigger or fiercer than Tegleth the Baazite whom I slew by the crystal waters of Erriad, and I will do likewise to this fellow!" Arrax roared like a wounded beast and lunged at Keniah, battering his shield with his sword, but Keniah held his ground and endured the

129

buffeting of Arrax, saying to him, "Your arm is strong Arrax, son of Ancyrus, but you have yet to move me. Now we shall see how you deal with my blows!" and in saying this he pounded Arrax with the face of his shield, throwing the noble brother of Ioclus to the ground. But Arrax became enraged, and his blood boiled hot within him, and brandishing his brazen sword he roared again at Keniah and threw himself upon the Marudan with such violence that Keniah was forced to give ground. Then Arrax cried with a great fury and struck the Vecantian shield of Keniah and split it in two straight down the middle. Keniah was speechless, for never had his great shield even been dented by any challenger, let alone fail him.

But Arrax's sword was shattered from the blow and he hurled it to the ground. Keniah struck at him with his blade, but hot-blooded Arrax deflected the blows with his great arms, hard as stone and round as cedar trunks. Then he pummeled the face and head of Keniah with his iron fists, knocking the helm from the Marudan's head into the dirt and driving his opponent to his knees. The Caeylonics gasped and cried out with awe, for Keniah panted heavily, and fear was in his eyes. Then Arrax took up a spear from one of his companions and thrust it into Keniah's side, piercing his liver and sending a shrieking howl up from the Marudan. He laid Keniah low and stood aloft upon him, his foot on his neck, and said, "Go to death now, dog, cursing the day that you thought to engage Arrax son of Ancyrus in combat," and having said this he lunged forth with his spear and gouged the throat of Keniah, spilling out his life upon the bloodied dirt before him. When the Marudans saw this, they all alike cried out in fear and fled into the woods, some this way and some that, only desiring to flee from Arrax. But Arrax gathered up the fragments of his shattered sword, the shield of Keniah which had split, the Marudan's marvelously wrought helm that he had pounded off with his fists, and the blade of Keniah, and these he took to be heirlooms of his house forever and displayed them in his noble hall alongside the shield of Tegleth whom he slew by the Erriad. Thus it is sung in the regions of Paros to this day whenever the exploits of Arrax and his house are recalled at the feasts which are yearly offered up in his memory:

Who is like unto Arrax the bold?
Who shattered the shield which Keniah did hold
He thought the Asylian in ease would he slay-

130

yet Arrax the Marudan in death did he lay.

Now evening was far spent, for it had been some time since midnight and a dense fog settled in the wood. Then it was that the din of battle was heard among the Marudan sentries at the outer edge of the clearing wherein was camped Adaran and his company, nigh unto five thousand men. Adaran was troubled in his heart and paced to and fro throughout the camp, consulting with Bula his advisor and awaiting word from Keniah and from Zeleth, whom he did not know had both been slain by Arrax, and also for word from the Kushites under Olrath and Negurac, both of whom had been slain along with the messenger Ribah when the Kushites had determined upon fleeing. Also present with Adaran were Mozarus of Nadare and Enech of Lyson, two valiant commanders of Caeylon. As Adaran and his captains paced the camp, a runner approached him with his garments rent and ashes on his head, and fell down before Adaran weeping. Adaran was wroth and said, "Stand, man, and tell us what causes you to weep so."

Then the man stood upon his feet and with great terror in his voice said, "The Asylians are assaulting the camp round about from all sides. Furthermore, Keniah the great captain has fallen, slain by Arrax brother of Ioclus in open battle and his men have all fled." Then Adaran trembled with rage and said the Bula, "Blow the horn! Rouse the camp! By Mardu, we shall chastize these foul fiends who strike in the shadows!" Then the horns were blown and the men of the encampment were raised from their slumber. And it was about the seventh hour of the night.

As the horns were blowing and the captains of Adaran debating stratagems and courses of action, Manissa led her Asylians in assaulting the southwestern side of the camp, and she was aided in this by long-haired Amyntas and bold Eridax while Arrax attacked the camp further north. The Marudans perceived their advance and strengthened their shields against them, and the Asylians charged forth out of the dark mists of the forest and crashed upon the Marudan shield wall with great force, sending a fearsome clang throughout the wood. Manissa, mounted on Ruah, directed her men, telling them where the line was weak and should be assaulted and where it was strong and from whence to draw back. She dashed this way and that upon the back of her tireless black steed, striking men down with the spear of Ioclus and

131

rallying her warriors. Terrible and beautiful she was to behold that fateful eve, glorious and comely in the moonlight but frighful and spattered with gore. She rode up and down the lines harrowing the Marudans and in doing so perceived that they were taking orders from one mounted officer, a captain named Irulah who bellowed commands from behind the lines. She thus spurred her horse onward, braved the whetted spears of the Marudans and leapt into their midst, growling like an enraged mountain lion, and taking aim at Irulah, let fly the mighty shaft of Ioclus. Her arm was powerful and her aim flawless; the shaft split the air with her throw and crashed into the breast of Irulah, shattering breastplate and bone alike, and throwing him from his horse. Then Manissa cried, "Three fine mares from the queen's stables to whoever retrieves for me my shaft!" This rallied the Asylians, for they all desired to recover the spear of Ioclus for their queen, and they roared and broke through the Marudan lines, slaying many in their charge and putting the rest to flight. But it was Arummnax of Orioön who recovered the spear and presented it to Manissa, and after the battle was ended she fulfilled her word concerning him and the mares.

Naross had come around the camp the longer way by means of circling to the north and attempted to assault it from the east, trapping Adaran between his own men and those of the queen. But it came to pass that his men came upon the legion of Omer the Fast, who had been wandering aimlessly in the wood for the better part of the day and had become hopelessly lost. When the Marudans perceived the Asylians upon them there was a desperate battle in the fog, man grappling with man in the dirt and many spears flying through the dank night mist, some striking friend instead of foe. The battle began to go poorly for the Asylians, and old Naross called a retreat. But Omer, who was the fastest of all men, dashed after Naross and said, "You shall not elude me as did your compatriot!" and he hurled his spear, a sturdy shaft of finest tamarisk wood created by the craftsmen of Koriath, and struck Naross between the shoulder blades as he was fleeing, so that he fell with his face to the dirt. The Asylian spearmen with Naross wept and fought to recover his body, but Omer drove them off and said, "Begone, vultures! This spoil is mine," and he knelt to strip the body of Naross.

But as Naross lay panting his life away in the dirt, he prayed, "By all the gods and the beard of Manx, grant me one last time to deal death to my enemies before I am enfolded in darkness." Having said this, he raised himself up and took hold of his spear in his blood-stained hands and turned and thrust it into the belly of Omer, who was kneeling near him. Omer cried out and doubled over, and when Naross withdrew the spear his guts came spilling out behind it. Thus died Omer the Fast. Then Naross said, "The sacred stag, the Lamassu, which meant blessing for the queen was a portent of woe for me. Yet at least I have preserved my honor," and having said this, collapsed onto the damp earth beside the pale body of Omer and gave up his spirit. Thus perished old Naross of the Great Throw, three years the junior of Ioclus, son of Ancyrus and wisest of all Asylian lords. The Marudans who had followed Omer and remained unsure of their location vanished away into the darkness, some to return to Adaran's camp, some to be picked off by the Asylians prowling the great trunks of the wood by night, few to ever return again to sun-drenched Caeylon and its endless skies of blue. But the Asylians who had been following Naross knew where they were and marched west, hoping to soon come upon the encampment of Adaran and attack his rear.

Now Manissa sighted that Marudan fires were being lit within the central encampment, and that officers and men were moving to and fro, and she said to her captains, "Adaran is on the move. The din of battle has alarmed him and he is forming ranks. We must strike him now, while we still have the darkness of night and while they are yet to be fully mustered." Then she sent her fastest runner northward to the men of Arrax, who had just finished routing the Marudans on the western edge of the Caeylonic camp following the slaying of Keniah. The servant said to Arrax, "My lord Arrax, Queen Manissa asks whether you are ready to put an end to Adaran and the Marudans?" Arrax clashed his sword to his shield and cried out, "For this purpose was I born." Then the servant said, "Therefore my Lady says go forth and begin the assault on the main camp, and may Fate be kind unto thee." Then hot-blooded Arrax formed up his men into companies of tens and hundreds and said to them, "Now we make the Marudans pay in blood for the Hall of Orix. Be fierce, my brethren, for only with such fierceness can we overcome this foe. Let every trembling knee cease and every weak hand be strengthened. Let the swords be drawn, spears cast, shields shattered and blood be spilled. Cruacha!" With one accord the Asylians hosts cried,

133

"Cruacha!" Then Arrax raised his gore-stained sword and called the march, and the hosts of Asylia moved east to engage Adaran.

Thus it was that in the black darkness of the night, around the third hour before dawn, hot-blooded Arrax at the head of four thousand Asylian spearmen charged the westernmost defenses of the Caeylonic camp, overrunning the picket with little effort and making great headway into the main center of the encampment. Cries rang throughout the Marudans' encampment, and Adaran was seized with fear. He sent Mozarus of Nadare and Enech of Lyson to rally the men at once and make a stand, and the two valiant captains of Caeylon managed to marshall some four thousand infantry with which to stop the assault of Arrax. The Asylians ran throughout the camp, setting fire to tents and spearing men as they tried to leap forth from their blankets. In this the Asylians jeered, for they recalled the noble sons of Ioclus, Masaros, Menelor and Eleth, who were speared to death as they leapt forth from their tents at the sound of battle. Many Marudans banded together in companies and charged the ranks of Arrax, but Arrax was overcome with bloodlust and raged through the Marudan ranks, his voice roaring like a bear. No blade held aloft against him could turn away his glittering sword, nor could any shield withstand his blows, the blows which smashed the shield of Keniah. Some Marudans hurled spears and javelins at him, but these struck his rugged flesh harmlessly, like so many sticks, and fell to the earth. The Marudan's cried, "He is possessed by some god," and fled before him. Everywhere Arrax turned he struck men down with his blade, killing scores of common men and many captains as well. And behind him came the Asylian hordes, crying "Cruacha!" and hurling their spears at whatsoever dared to move before them, slaying in the shadows.

But Mozarus and Enech brought their legions to bear upon Arrax and stopped his progress, for they had in their ranks many archers who with one accord fired volleys into the Asylians and forced them to cease their advance, for the arrows rained down upon them and sorely harassed them, and many men were slain, among them Iulos, who had been a friend of Manissa's brother Menelor from youth. Mozarus sent word to Adaran that Arrax's men were stopped in their advance and begged him to bring up his reinforcements, but as the runners left to find Adaran, Manissa attacked the clearing from the southwest, and with her were long-haired Amyntas and rash Eridax, each commanding two thousand men. They charged into the camp from the black woods, coming like spectres from the mist, bearing down upon the legions of Mozarus and Enech from the flanks and shredding scores of men with their bronze-capped spears. Eridax sighted out Enech who was bringing up the rear of the column and cast his spear at him. A fatal throw! The point struck Enech in the throat and felled him, and he gurgled and thrashed his life away upon the black dirt of the forest floor. Rank upon rank of bearded Asylian and Cadarasian warriors, teeth bared in rage and spears seeking blood, poured into the encampment and smashed the flanks of the Marudan lines, tearing and slicing and piercing at every turn. Then the Marudans realized their folly, for if they turned to fend off the pressing attack of Eridax, Amyntas and Manissa then they exposed their flank to the rage of Arrax, who slew men as one takes the scythe to grass at harvest time; but if they made a stand against Arrax, the armies of Manissa sliced their company from the flank.

Mozarus sought to rally his men and split them into two, so as to defend against raging Arrax, Manissa and the other lords at once. But many more Asylians flooded into the camp from the woods and hurled their spears into the Marudan column, so that the night air was thick with biting spearheads that stung and pierced the Marudans like so many wasps. Thus it was that a stray spear struck Mozarus as he called orders to his column, lodging itself in his ribs and piercing his lung. He tried to speak to his captains but could not, and his breath failed him. One of his captains, a young man inexperienced in battle, said, "I will draw the spear out, my lord." Then he plucked the spear forth from the ribs of Mozarus. When he did so Mozarus let forth a great cry, and a stream of crimson blood came pouring from the wound. The stream could not be staunched, though many men aided him, and he died there on the ground in the arms of his aides. When he died, the hosts of Maruda were left leaderless.

But Adaran had rallied all the men left in the camp, those who had not gone out with Mozarus and Enech and many more who had fled into the camp from the outer regions, along with stragglers coming in from Omer's legion, who told him that Omer had been killed. Then Bula said, "My lord, if Omer is fallen, as well as Mozarus and Enech as seems to be true, then we have lost all our captains and generals! The whole of the battle falls on us!" Adaran scoffed and said, "I may not be so fortunate as to catch that Asylian queen in my sights, nor may I find Arrax under my blade, but by all the gods, my sword will not fall to the ground before I make some Asylian bastard pay for what has occurred tonight! Come then, Bula! For either we wreak doom upon the Asylians or we embrace our own." Adaran donned his red war cape and his finely wrought helm and went off to engage the Asylians. Bula followed behind, remembering the words of Arahaz.

The camp was in an uproar and was thrown into confusion, for the legions of Mozarus and Enech had broken up and the battle became an open melee, Asylian fighting Marudan man to man beneath the pale starlight, men falling bloodied and wounded into the damp earth and life ebbing away at the end of sword or spear, the night air reeking with gore. The Marudans fought fiercely, for they struggled for their very lives, and many valiant Asylians were slain, among them Neraulos of Paros, a favorite of Arrax, and Thareth of An-Gihar, a famed spearman and a friend of the sons of Naross, who was struck in the heart by a Marudan spear and died at once. But the Asylians fought with great fury, while the fear of the Caeylonics made their own weak, so that everywhere Asylian prevailed over Marudan. But as the battle raged, Adaran himself came forth with his sword borne aloft and his great red cloak upon his shoulders, leading behind him every able bodied Marudan left within the camp, and with one accord they charged the Asylians and cast their spears at them, raining death upon the troops of Arrax and Manissa and felling many. But when they had discharged their volley, the Asylians rallied and charged their ranks, and the dark woods were filled with the sounds of shield crashing upon shield and weapons clanging in the night air. But none dared assault Adaran, for his stature was great and his countenance fearful.

Yet rash Eridax said in his heart, "Perhaps it is granted to me to fell this Marudan tyrant," and he went forth and did battle with him. But alas, the heart of Eridax spoke deceit, for Adaran deflected his blows and smote him with his great sword, slicing his flesh from shoulder to stomach and felling him to the ground, bloodied and panting. Adaran would have finished him, had not the followers of Eridax dragged him away before Adaran could land his next blow, thus rescuing the Lord of Cadaras.

The Caeylonics fought hard, and long-haired Amyntas tried in vain to break their lines, though he slew many of them. He called to Manissa, "My lady, this Caeylonic lord gives them power to continue the fight and our men are weary. We shall have to retire for the evening and be content with out victory thus far." But Manissa said, "If we cease now, we shall never have such a chance again. Therefore, press on, though you and your men be sunk down with weariness." When Adaran perceived the Asylians were wearied, he pressed the attack even hotter, and with his own blade came forth at the fore of the Caeylonic ranks and slew twenty men of Arrax's company. Thus the Asylians were sorely pressed.

But at that time, the legion of Naross (who had been lately slain by Omer) came forth into the camp from the east, and seeing the Marudans hotly engaged with their kinsmen, threw themselves upon the Marudan rear, thus pinning Adaran between the ranks of Manissa and the lords to the west and the legions of Naross on the east. When the Marudans saw this, panic spread among them and they began to give ground to the Asylians, and finally turned to flee when the spears of the men of Naross began striking them. Thus the legions of Adaran began to melt away, though he cursed and raged about and threatened them with all manner of punishments. Yet nothing could induce them to stay. Then Bula said, "Master, the field is lost. Cede victory and flee, for we are encompassed about on all sides and cannot win this engagement. Alas, it is as Arahaz warned." At the mention of Arahaz, Adaran grew enraged and turned and struck off the head of Bula with his sword, so that it tumbled some distance on the ground. But many of the Caeylonics fled into the darkness of the woods while others surrendered to the Asylians, and others still pressed the battle.

Then Arrax caught sight of Adaran and lunged for him and would not fight with any great or small save Adaran. When Adaran saw him coming, he said, "Who is this man of might with hair black as a raven and sword reeking with gore? By Mardu, his body looks like it has been sculpted from fine marble, and the very fire of the deep is in his eyes. The ground quakes at his approach and men fall away like women before him. This can be none other than Arrax, of whom many tales are sung even among the Marudans!" He thus drew his sword and prepared to engage Arrax, but when the Asylian lord of Paros came upon him, hot for blood and with merciless vengeance in his eyes, the heart of Adaran failed. His knees became like water and his stomach dropped like a stone; his hands trembled and his commanding voice left him, and his men melted away about him, so that he stood alone before cruel Arrax, who had doom in his eyes and had made a solemn oath to bring Adaran down in death. It is sung in

137

the songs of Asylia how Adaran before Arrax was like a boy before a god, so fierce was the lord of Paros in his bloodlust.

Thus it was that Adaran was overcome with fear and turned and fled before Arrax. But Arrax pursued him and panted after him and would not be stopped, till he came upon Adaran and seized him by his cloak of red. Then he said, "You shall surely die, Adaran!" and struck at him with his sword. But Adaran pulled himself loose, so that Arrax cut only half of his cloak from him. Thus Adaran fled, and Arrax was left holding half the cloak of Adaran in his hand.

But Arrax pursued him and panted after him and would not be stopped, till he came upon Adaran and seized him by the locks of long, dark hair hanging out from behind his helm. Then he said, "You shall surely die, Adaran!" and struck at him with his sword. But Adaran pulled himself loose, so that Arrax cut only the locks of his hair from him. Thus Adaran fled, and Arrax was left holding the black locks of Adaran in his hand.

But Arrax pursued him and panted after him and would not be stopped, till he came upon Adaran and seized him by his beard. Then he said, "You shall surely die, Adaran!" and struck at him with his sword. But Adaran pulled himself loose, so that Arrax cut only half of his beard from him. Thus Adaran fled, and Arrax was left holding half the beard of Adaran in his hand.

He would have pursued Adaran further, but Manissa sent a message to him saying, "Will you abandon the army for the sake of one man? Turn from your pursuit and return unto us, so that we may put an end to these Marudans and secure victory for ourselves and our kin forever." So Arrax turned back from pursuing Adaran and returned to Manissa, though he brought forth with him the piece of the cloak of Adaran, the locks of hair severed from his head and the portion of beard sliced from his face. These became the most precious heirlooms in all his house.

But the Asylians ran throughout the camp freely, looting and burning and slaying all who put up resistance. Whoever was not dead among the Marudans fled into the woods, and many threw down their arms and offered themselvs up to Manissa, and as many as did so were pardoned and spared. As morning broke upon the woods of Arcoria the smoke of the Marudan camp could be seen ascending up from many miles around, and the gray dawn brought with it the gentle light of morn, which illumined the great clearing that had been the Marudan camp and exposed to the sight

138

of the Asylians how fierce the battle had been. When the Asylians saw the field of battle they wept and feared their own rage, for so great was the slaughter that there was not one spot of open earth that was bared to the sky, for there was no foot of ground that did not have at least one dead body upon it. Asylian warriors and Marudan captives alike strolled amongst the dead, gazing and marvelling, saying, "Look! There lies the body of brave Enech who was struck down by the hand of Manissa herself!" or, "See there! This is the spot where the shield of Keniah was shattered." And they said many like things. The head of Bula was also found. The Marudan captives were set to work accounting for the dead, and when the entire field of the clearing and the surrounding forests had been examined, it was reported that eighteen thousand Marudans had been slain, and of the Asylians less than five hundred.

Then Manissa found the golden chair which Adaran had been accustomed to sit upon in his tent. Upon this she stood aloft and summoned the armies before her. She was glorious and terrible to behold, her single braid of hair hanging bloodied upon her back, her green cloak matted with mud and encrusted with blood and her hands mired in gore and dirt. When the Asylian forces surrounded her, she spoke to them, saying, "This night we have won a glorious victory, one that shall make the very throne of Belthazre tremble and shall be remembered and sung of from this day until the very ending of the world! After this eve, every warrior who hears the names of Arrax, Amyntas, Eridax and Manissa will quake in fear and marvel, saying, 'They led the pride of the Caeylonic army into the wood, and none came forth again.' And yet it is bought with great tragedy, for word has come that our kinsman and my uncle, wise Naross, fell under the spear of Omer. He goes to be with his brother, Ioclus, my father of happy memory, and all our kin who went before us. But the struggle is not yet over, for Adaran our foe has fled, and with him many more. Let us make a pursuit and drive them utterly from the land, lest they take some position as a foothold and fortify it and send for reinforcements from Caeylon." Then all the men crashed their spears to their shields and cried out, "Yea! Cruacha e Manissé!" But the Marudan prisoners were taken south into the land of Lugaria and sold to the Lugarians to work in the mines in that region, so that few ever returned unto Caeylon again.

Manissa marshalled her people and marched eastward out

139

of the Arcorian woods, leaving the bodies of the Caeylonics where they fell. They marched with great haste, as a leopard pursuing its prey, and came forth from the densest part of the wood after only three days, neither eating nor stopping to rest. When they came forth, Alscetor of Lugaria greeted them there with three thousand stallions and many provisions, saying, "We saw the smoke of the Marudans camp and perceived that you had won a great victory. Therefore, we made haste to come hither with these horses and supplies to aid you in your pursuit." Manissa thanked them graciously and sent forth Arrax and Amyntas with three thousand picked men to make a pursuit, for Alscetor said, "We saw Adaran and several hundred Marudans come this way not two days ago heading east across the Cyrian Highlands. Furthermore, his look was odd, for he had but half a beard." When Arrax heard this, he made great haste and mounted his steed, charging off across the highlands in pursuit, three thousand battle hardened Asylians behind him with spears angry for vengeance.

Now Adaran had come upon some horses wandering wild in Arcoria and seized them and fled eastward, his cloak torn, his hair shorn and wearing but half his beard. Behind him were several hundred Marudan soldiers, some with horses but most on foot, some wounded and some not, all fleeing east. Many of these were overcome by the horsemen of Arrax, and as many as fell behind or were found by Arrax were slain upon the highlands, for Arrax could not be constrained to show pity unless Manissa was present to restrain his wrath. Four days after this Adaran rode into Asylia, which was being governed by Arahaz. He found the people there dwelling in peace, for they were rebuilding the walls of the city and were taking inventory of the fields and lands seized from the Asylians. Adaran came straight away to see Arahaz and said, "Flee, flee! The Asylians come behind me hot for blood. Flee!" He stayed no more to speak with Arahaz, but mounted a new horse and fled away eastward, hoping within three days to cross the Erriad. But the Marudans dwelling in the region of Asylia panicked, and some fled to the countryside, but most prepared for battle the best they could, for the city of Asylia was still not fully rebuilt. Arahaz managed the defense, though there was not much that could be done and a great fear fell upon everyone.

On the second day after the departue of Adaran, the men of Arrax and Amyntas came to Asylia by dawn and saw the Marudans dwelling in it. Then Arrax trembled in rage and said, "Let us drive these foreigners out and send them to the abyss!" So they charged the city and assaulted it, and the Marudans dwelling there made no defense but fled, some carrying their belongings, others not. The Asylians overcame the light defenses and rode throughout the streets of their once proud capital, routing any who put up a defense and hurling cruel spears at whatever man was so foolish as to be caught in the street. Long-haired Amyntas was full of zeal for the Hall of Orix, which he had last seen when the Marudans had set fire to it. He rode forth to the hill of the Hall, where a stately dwelling in the Caeylonic style was in the process of being erected, and where was residing Arahaz, ruler of the city. When Arahaz saw Amyntas riding down the lanes towards the hill, he remembered him as the one who had overthrown Danath Hered by way of the cistern that sat in the center of the fortress. Then Arahaz lamented and said, "My evil deeds have come back upon me." He washed his face and put on fresh robes of linen, and taking his walking stick, went to the gate of the building to await the coming of Amyntas. When Amyntas came riding up the lane, spear held aloft, he saw Arahaz standing in the doorway and knew him. Then he spurred his horse forward and rode with great fury towards Arahaz, his long hair blowing about him and his teeth gnashed in fury. Arahaz held his arms aloft, baring his breast, and fell to his knees in the doorway upon the approach of Amyntas. Amyntas rode hard upon the threshold of the house and hurled his death-bringing spear at Arahaz. It struck Arahaz squarely in the chest, tearing through the delicate linens and crushing his breastbone with a great crash. He was pierced straight through, so that the cruel spearhead came forth from his back and the delicate white linens became soaked with blood. Arahaz did not utter a cry or a single word, but fell over dead upon the threshold of the building. Then Amyntas set fire to the dwelling of Arahaz and burned his body within it. Thus perished Arahaz, captain of Caeylon.

But Arrax and his men rode forth upon the plains, harrowing the fleeing Marudans. Arrax had commanded that every able bodied man they were to kill, but women and children were to be taken away to serve the people of Asylia. So they pursued them and struck them all along the plains, from Asylia along the road that leads to Kerion for the better part of a day and a night. Now Arrax rode on ahead of the rest of the men, for he was still seeking Adaran in hopes of slaying him. But by and by as he came down the road he saw a fresh spring by the wayside and thought to stop and refresh himself before continuing the pursuit. And upon drinking from the stream he lifted up his eyes and beheld a Marudan maiden weeping in the grass nearby. He same unto her and said, "Maiden, why do you weep?" She looked up and he saw that she was beautiful, for her hair was dark like his own and her flesh was the color of olive, and her eyes were gentle and almond shaped. And the heart of Arrax was smitten with desire. She said, "O cruel master of Asylia, how can you say 'Why do you weep?' You yourself know very well, for this day I have been bereaved of my husband, a merchant of Caeylon, who was slain upon the road while fleeing from Asylia." Arrax said, "You know who I am?" The maiden said, "You are cruel Arrax, deadly in war, bitter in victory and ever bent upon slaughter and destruction."

Arrax said, "I do not deny that I am fierce to my enemies and a fear to those who stand against me. But I am also gentle and compassionate to my kin and loving to those who show me honor. As for your husband, I suppose he would not have grieved had Adaran returned with news that Arrax had been slain? Would he not have rejoiced and made merry that the Asylian barbarians had been defeated? Nay, I do not pity him, for he received his due. But tell me, what name are you called by?"

She scorned him and said, "Oh most hateful of men to me, whether you should carry me away to your savage home or cut my flesh with your cruel blade or strike me with your bloody and merciless fists, I will not tell thee my name. Leave me be, that I may die here by this spring."

Arrax said, "Far be it from me that I should do what you have spoken, or leave you to die here. I pray thee, tell me your name, for you are beautiful and I desire to know how to call thee. I swear, I will by no means harm you."

She said, "I will never tell you, for you are an angry and violent man, moved by your passions and quick to slay, and how do I know that some evil will not befall me despite your word? I do not wish for you to know me, most loathsome and violent of men."

Then Arrax, carried off by his heart, threw down his sword and knelt before the maiden and said, "Maiden, have no fear of my anger, for from the moment I saw thee I have been smitten with love for thee. Therefore, hear me now: I swear, by the beard of Manx, the good name of my Queen Manissa, and by all the gods of Maruda and Asylia, if you should tell me your name, that I will put up my sword and spear forever and never make war again nor strike another man in anger till the very ending of my days. I call heaven and earth to witness against me if I should violate this most sacred oath which I have sworn before thee."

When she saw him kneeling before her with his sword cast into the grass and thought on the mighty oath he had sworn, her heart was moved and she relented, and said to him, "I am a maid of Caeylon, born in the great city in the shadow of the royal palace. My name is Sammurah." When Arrax heard this name, he grimaced and said, "Despite thy beauty, Sammurah, your name is hateful to Asylian ears and hard to pronounce. Therefore I will call you Erissa. Henceforth you shall no longer be called Sammurah, but Erissa." Then Arrax took Sammurah, called Erissa, back to his own city of Paros and there was wed to her. And he became a man of peace from that day forward. In later days, Erissa bore to Arrax a single son, Erogel, and Erogel took to wife Analissa of Cadarasia and begat a daughter, Anaxandra, who in later days was queen over all the peoples of Elabaea.

But there were many men of Caeylon who eluded Arrax and dwelt in the wilderness, and in the following days, many of these and the soldiers of Adaran who had escaped the Arcorian Wood came forth from the wilds and asked Manissa for clemency. She granted this and gave them the environs surrounding Asylia to the south and west, going as far as the Cyrian Highlands. Their descendants dwell there to this day as nomads and are called the *Manruthim*.

But Adaran fled across the Erriad, and Amyntas turned back from pursuing him to return west to welcome the queen back into Asylia. Adaran meanwhile cast off his Marudan apparel in the wilds south of Cadaras, for fear of being seized, and adopted the garb of a simple herdsman. In such garb he came unto Anentora in the third week after fleeing Arcoria and from thence proceeded to Caeylon once his beard had grown back. When his coming was made known in Caeylon, Narússa the queen went unto Belthazre her husband who was strolling in the orchards and said, "My king, live forever! The grand army of Adaran has returned from Asylia!" When Belthazre heard this, he was greatly excited and said, "Where is it?" And she said, "It is mustered in the courtyard of the palace." So Belthazre had himself washed and anointed and donned the regal crown of the house of Anathar and went forth with many nobles and officials into the courtyard to greet the army. But when he arrived he found only Adaran alone, humbled and disheveled, standing in the courtyard. Then Narússa said, "Behold, the army of Adaran!" When Belthazre understood what had happened and heard of the loss of the grand army, he was filled with rage and had Adaran cast into the dungeon beneath the palace to be reserved in chains until he could think of what to do with him.

Being greatly angered, he retired to his palace and brooded about his bedchamber. Then Narússa came unto him mockingly and said, "And what mighty designs does the king devise now for the conquest of Elabaea?" At the mention of Elabaea he flew into a rage and grasped his wife by the hair and said, "What designs have I, you say? Only one - a design I ought to have carried out long ago!" Then he dragged Narússa by the hair to the door of his chamber and brought her to the top of a mighty staircase, and then he hurled her with great violence down the stair. The stairs were very high and the king had thrown her with great force, so that her body was broken and her bones shattered as she fell at the foot of the staircase. There she perished on the hard stone floor gasping her last breaths unheard and unpitied. But Belthazre retired to his room and took his afternoon nap which he was wont to take each day.

But Adaran he left to linger in prison for a long while, and after four months of imprisonment he brought him forth and had him hanged on some gallows that he constructed in the courtyard of the palace, so that Adaran died dangling over the same spot where he had returned from Asylia to stand before the king alone.

When news reached Lugaria that the Marudans had been destroyed from the land, there was great rejoicing, and all of the women and children and infirm who had taken refuge with the Lugarians fled northward and came upon the army of Manissa returning east near the grove of Aialon. Then there was much rejoicing and weeping, for wives were brought together with their men and children with parents. Then Manissa and ordered a great feast and a festival for seven days to commemorate the victory and the reunion of the men with their families. But by and by, as the first days of autumn came turning the green grasses of the plains brown, Manissa came unto the city of Asylia and found it desolate. All the Asylians wept for the burning of the Hall of Orix and the destruction that had been wrought there. There Manissa fulfilled her vow and cut from her head the great braid of her hair which she had worn in battle and burnt it in sacrifice before the ruins of the Hall. And all the people put ashes on their heads and wept.

Then Manissa came unto Paros and wintered there in the house of Arrax, her uncle. There were the funeral rites for Naross son of Ancyrus carried out, and the body of Naross was brought and laid to rest in a splendid tomb in Paros which Arrax his brother constructed for him. But when the days of winter were complete, Manissa crossed the Erriad with great fanfare on the first day of spring and came unto Cadarasia and was welcomed into the city with much rejoicing. She confirmed Eridax as lord of that realm and received his homage. At that time also, Hadrior returned from Baris in Cyrenaica and found Manissa at Cadaras, and she rejoiced greatly to see her brother-in-law, though she was sorely grieved at his injuries which were given to him in the pit of Ochu; and all the lords of Asylia and Cadarasia listened in wonder to the tale of Hadrior concerning this.

Because Asylia had been destroyed, Manissa set up her throne at Cadarasia and reigned as queen there from the beginning of the fifth year of her reign until her passing from the world. Thus peace returned to the west, and as the days passed the blood and dirt vanished from the nails of Manissa and she became again gentle and delicate and donned the regal gowns of a noblewoman of Asylia. Her hair also returned, and was worn in intricate braids upon the back of her head. In the summer of that year she was wed to Amyntas, Lord of Kerion, and unto him she bore seven children: first, a girl Mariammné, then followed six sons, first Baldor, who afterwards became a mighty warrior, exceeding even Arrax in fury; then Hazer, who was a composer of poems and songs; Necho and Elphas, twins and men of renown; then Secum, of whom it was said that the wisdom of Naross had returned, for he was wise and gave counsel to many great men; finally was born Perior, who roamed the countryside like a wildman and had a great strength that rivaled that of the giants whom he warred with in the hill country to the west.

Then there was peace in the land, and all came and did homage to Manissa and called her Queen of All Elabaeans. Asylia was rebuilt in the west, but as the queen reigned from Cadarasia, the Asylians said, "Let us make our home east of the Erriad to be near our beloved queen," and so many of them moved east, making their homes in the environs of Cadarasia, so that Cadaras grew larger while Asylia diminished in size. Thus Cadarasia was built up and made glorious, and the city was fortified and made strong, even greater than it had been in the days of Garba. In the second year of her queenship in Cadaras (being the seventh of her reign), she began the reconstruction of the Temple of Mironna, which was completed in the ninth year of her reign. It was a marvel to behold, and men came from as far away as Elam and Ituria to see it, and when they beheld it, they exclaimed, "This is the greatest temple that has ever stood in Elabaea since the days when Laban wandered west and settled these regions." And all gave glory to Manissa. Though Belthazre did not admit himself to have been defeated, nor did he formally revoke any of the edicts of his earlier reign or those of his father Dathan, he nevertheless came no more into the west and ceased pursuing war with the Elabaeans for the rest of his days. In later days the Marudans again became well disposed towards the Elabaeans and came again into the west in peace as merchants and traders and again gave sons and daughters in marriage to the Elabaeans and took the sons and daughter of the Elabaeans in marriage. But as the kingdoms of the west were strong under Manissa, never again did the Marudans attempt to oppress them. And both Maruda and Cadarasia grew wealthy because of the trade between those two lands. Then Manissa waxed strong, and Epidymia waned, and the kingdom of Cadaras was exteneded northwards into the hinterlands of Epidymia bordering the Gihon Valley. The people of Bados came and did homage to Manissa as well, and the Lugars of Karanus made treaties of friendship and alliance with her all her days, as did the wildmen of Ituria. But King Endumion of Cyrenaica remianed hostile to Manissa and would not be reconciled to her for as long as she lived. And all her days Manissa ruled justly and guided the peoples of Asylia and Cadarasia in wisdom and goodness, and her husband, Lord Amyntas, was placed over all the armies of the west, as Arrax had vowed to make war no more. Every year she reigned she increased in splendor and glory until she excelled Osseia in beauty and Naross in wisdom, and it was said of her, "In Manissa the blood of Orix, son of Manx, lives again, for she is more divine than human." Men traveled from as far away as Kush and Lyson to gaze upon her and hear the words of wisdom which dripped like honey continually from her lips. And all the deeds of Manissa, of her righteous judgments, the victories of her captains, the wisdom which she gave to her people and the miraculous signs which occured under her reign, are they not written in the annals of the Kings of Manis?

Manissa reigned eighteen years, four from the death of Ioclus to the victory in the Arcorian, and fourteen years from Adaran's defeat and her enthronement in Cadarasia. But in her later years Manissa was restless, for her kingdom being at peace, she longed again to see the wilds of the western lands where she had roamed in her youth, and also because she bore in her soul the desire to see again one of the stags of Agenor, the Lamassu, which she had gazed upon twice in her early years. Therefore she went often on progresses through the countryside with a small retinue, including Amytas her husband and some other servants and kin. They would ride west of the Erriad into the empty fields and hillocks of Asylia and hunt fox or hart and come again unto

Cadaras with much meat and great rejoicing.

The last summer of her reign, when she was forty years old, Manissa went west unto the wild lands south of Asylia and came to a wilderness which she knew, and said to her retinue, "By the gods, I have seen this place before, but its name escapes me." Then Amyntas said, "My lady, this is the wilderness of Enna in the region of En Ganar, which borders upon Lugaria to the south of Asylia." Then Manissa said, "By the beard of Manx! Enna! Blessed Enna, where my sister Osseia once fled the envy of Belthazre and wept by the great terebinth tree. How strange that I should come again to this place, of which the last time I was here was I but a maiden, and the hand of Maruda heavy upon our land." Then she rode about and came unto the terebinth of Osseia in Enna and wept before it, saying, "Behold how I, even I, have grown older and nearer to the grave! Many of my kin are now departed, not only my brothers and sisters who died young, but even hardy Arrax and bold Eridax, companions of war, have preceded me in death. And yet the wilds of Enna and the terebinth of Osseia remain ever fresh as they looked the day I bid Osseia farewell from this place when Ioclus was in counsel with his lords over whether or not to take up spears against Belthazre. Flesh withers and fades and is blown to the winds, and whither goes the soul of man nobody can say. But the earth and sky endure forever, and serve to call to mind how fleeting are the days of man." Then they returned from the terebinth of Osseia in Enna and came again unto Cadaras, but ever after the heart of the queen roamed restlessly and could not be stilled.

In the early autumn of that year, when the land was still dry and warm and the leaves had not yet begun to turn, Manissa said to her husband Amyntas, "Let us again go forth on the hunt one last time before the coming of the snows." So she donned her green cloak and took with her the mighty spear of Ioclus and went forth on Ruah, who by this time was greatly advanced in age but was still swift and powerful; with the queen came Amyntas, Baldor her eldest son, and several servants and sons of different nobles. They crossed the Erriad and went northwest into the fertile regions south of the Gihon Valley, where in ages past Ioclus had chased the great boar with Ancryus, his father. When they had been on the hunt for six days and had not caught sight of any creature, neither hart nor fox nor boar, Manissa said, "Let us camp by the banks of the Sehu for one more night and if we see nothing on the following day we

148

shall return to Cadaras." And this seemed good to those with her.

But behold! That evening, as the sun waned beyond the western hills and the sky was pink over the land, Manissa went forth to lead Ruah to the Sehu to drink. There she looked up and beheld one of the great stags, the Lamassu, standing before her. It was greater and more glorious than she had remembered, and her flesh trembled when she beheld it, for it cast a pale shimmer over everything round about for some distance. Her breath stole from her, and her heart was set aflame. She said, "You shall not elude me this time, sacred beast! I shall have thee!" Then she grasped her spear and leapt upon Ruah, and the stag burst into a great run and set off along the eastern course of the Sehu going northward. Manissa cried and urged Ruah onward, and they fled from the camp. Then Amyntas saw her fleeing and cried, "Our queen is on the chase! Let us all go forth with her!" So the retinue saddled their horses and pursued Manissa and the Lamassu.

But the faster Manissa urged on Ruah in the chase, the further ahead the stag galloped, until it seemed to be almost flying over ground at marvelous strides. But Manissa was unwilling to be parted from the stag a third time and urged Ruah onward with ever greater vehemence, until sweat was pouring from the neck of her steed. Her party followed close behind, but Manissa rode so fast that soon all fell behind save Baldor her son and Amyntas her husband. She pursued the stag northward into Epidymia as the sun fell, and she trailed the stag all that night northward across the broad and pleasant plains and orchards of that land, riding hard beneath the moonlight, the Lamassu in front, herself on its heels, and Amyntas and Baldor someways behind her. The Epidymians slept and slumbered in their homes in the quiet of the night and knew not that the Queen of Elabaea and the sacred Lamassu passed through their land. So swiftly did they run that they passed through the entire region of Epidymia in but a single night, so that as the sun dawned over the eastern hills they had passed northward out of Epidymia into the environs of the great forest of Zurlina, which ascends upward over many miles and until one comes to the great mountains of the north.

Then Baldor called to his father and said, "I am wearied from riding all night long and my horse is near death. I must break off the pursuit, my father." So Baldor collapsed and rested, fatigued with riding and with much grief. Amyntas alone pursued Manissa northward into the marches of Zurlina. Manissa urged Ruah on, though he was greatly exhausted, and the stag darted up into the tangled woods that mark the southern limits of Zurlina. Here Ruah collapsed of fatigue under Manissa, and breathing his last, slumped over in death. But Manissa did not even cease at this, for she leapt forth from him and pursued the stag on foot, treading swiftly and leaping over brambles and fallen trees, hot on the trail of the Lamassu. But Amyntas followed close behind, and spurred his horse onward into the tangled brush, calling forth, "Manissa! My dearest wife! Why have you so abandoned us? Return, for our hearts are sick with worry." But she called back and said, "My beloved, I am carried away by something beyond my strength, and I know not how this shall end. Fare thee well." Then she cast forth the spear of Ioclus into the brush (for her arms were heavy from holding it) and began acsending the hills that lead one up into Zurlina, her eyes fixed on the Lamassu which ran ever upward some distance in front of her. Amyntas followed until the underbrush was such that he had to dismount, and then he pursued on foot. He came unto the spot where the spear of Ioclus had been cast into the weeds and marvelled that Manissa should so lightly throw away such a treasured heirloom, or that she should pursue such a beast with no weapon. He grasped the spear and continued to pursue her, though he was greatly wearied and stumbled many times.

Manissa ascended the forested hills of Zurlina and came unto a great ascent, like a great rocky stair on the side of a mountain. The area was quite high, and a dense mist settled over the place, but she still perceived the stag dashing ever upwards before her, and so she gave pursuit, panting with longing. Amyntas cried after her, "My love! My love!" and summoned all his strength, and making a great leap, came forward and caught up with Manissa, such that as she ran he put forth his hand and grasped the hem of her green cloak, the cloak which she had worn in the wilderness when fleeing from Lissus and had donned ever since. He clutched the cloak and would not be parted from her, crying, "Don't forsake us, my lady!" But she pressed onward, and the cloak ripped from her back and Amyntas was left alone kneeling in the mist with the cloak of Manissa in his hand, the last relic she left on the earth. Freed from his hand, she dashed ever upward, her brown and yellow hair blowing behind her, until she passed further up into the mist covered mountain and was lost from his sight. So Amyntas clung to the cloak of Manissa and wept bitterly. Then he gathered the cloak and the spear of Ioclus and passed back through Epidymia with great bitterness, mourning and striking his breast all the way to Cadarasia. But Ruah he buried there at the foot of the ascent to Zurlina, and the tomb of Ruah can still be seen there to this day. Then a great storm burst forth upon the land, such as had not been since the eve when Gygas had betrayed Ioclus upon the slopes of Lissus, and Amyntas returned to Cadaras drenched in the chill autumn rain and still clutching the green cloak of his queen.

When Amyntas returned to Cadarasia and bore the strange tidings of what he had seen, there was great mourning and lamentation throughout all of the land, for Manissa never came again unto her people nor was ever sighted after that among the sons of men. A great period of mourning was decreed in Cadarasia and all the cities of Elabaea, and people everywhere mourned and wept for the Maid of Asylia. Thus they did for forty days, until the time of mourning for Manissa Queen of Elabaea was ended.

Appendix A: Glossary of Important Persons and Places from the *Tale of Manaeth*

Adaran- Caeylonic general sent west to conquer Manissa; defeated in the Arcorian Wood.

Aenon- Son-in-law of Garba, killed at Ehuiel.

Agenor- Titan who planted the Arcorian wood.

Alscetor- Lugarian emissary and ally of Manissa.

Amyntas- Lord of Paros, Asylian war-chief and later husband of Manissa.

Anathar- First king of Maruda, semi-legendary.

Ancyrus- Father of Ioclus, Naross and Arrax.

An Erras- Plains west of the Erriad where Manissa won a great victory over Tegleth.

An Hered- Region east of Cadarasia where the Marudans first came into contact with the Elabaeans.

Arahaz- Captain of Belthazre; chief of Caeylonic forces in the west before the coming of Adaran.

Arrax- Uncle of Manissa and Asylian war-chief

Baldor- Eldest son of Manissa and Amyntas.

Belthazre- King of Caeylon, oppressor of the Elabaeans.

Bula- Aide of Adaran.

Cadar- A brook outside of Cadarasia.

Cadarasia- The great city of the Cadarasians east of Asylia, used interchangeably with Cadaras.

Caeylon- Greater Maruda; Maruda plus its conquered provinces. Used interchangeably with Maruda in the *Tale*.

Cruachan- Hill in Asylia where Manissa was crowned Queen.

Danath Hered- The chief Marudan fortress in Elabaea; destroyed by Manissa.

Dathan- Caeylonic king who put Elabaea under tribute and built Danath Hered.

Eilia- Asylian maiden; slain by order of Narússa.

Elabaea- Caeylonic name for all the western lands, including Asylia, Cadarasia, Epidymia and Ituria.

Eleth- Brother of Manissa; slain at Lissus.

Endumion- King of Cyrenaica who fed Karyon and Hadrior to Ochu.

Enna- Wild region between Asylia and Lugaria. Osseia hid here at En Ganar.

Epidymia- Powerful kingdom north of Cadarasia.

Eriar- Mythical mountain at the top of the world; abode of Manx.

Eridax- Asylian warrior who became lord of Cadarasia.

Erriad- Brook dividing Asylia from Cadarasia.

Garba- Lord of Cadarasia; brother-in-law of Ioclus.

Gihon- Great river northeast of Asylia.

Grianne- Wife of Ioclus and sister of Garba.

Gygas- Son of the lord of Gela; betrayer of Ioclus.

Hadrior- Brother-in-law of Manissa and Asylian war-chief.

Hall of Orix- Seat of Asylian rule.

Ioclus- Lord of Asylia and father of Manissa; slain at Lissus by the Marudans.

Keniah- Marudan general slain by Arrax.

Laban- Patriarch of all the peoples of Elabaea.

Lamassu- Great stags of Agenor.

Lissus- Hilly region in southern Ituria where Ioclus' house was wiped out.

Manaeth- Birth name of Manissa.

Manissa- Daughter of Ioclus, Queen of Asylia and heroine of the *Tale*.

Manx- One of the chief gods of Asylia.

Mardu- Chief Marudan god and patron of Caeylon.

Masaros- Eldest son of Ioclus; slain at Lissus.

Menelor- Son of Ioclus; slain at Lissus.

Naross- Uncle of Manissa and Asylian war-chief.

Narússa- Wife of Belthazre.

Paros- Asylian city east of the Erriad ruled by Amyntas.

Ochu- Cyrenaican water creature.

Orianna- Ancestress of Manissa; bore Orix by Manx.

Orix- Ancestor of Manissa, founded Asylia.

Osseia- Eldest and most beautiful daughter of Ioclus; sister of Manissa; died at Lissus.

Rammeth- Brother of Eridax; captured and slain at Danath Hered.

Ruah- The black horse of Manissa, a gift to her from Arrax.

Saraeth- Lame sister of Manissa and wife of Hadrior, slain at Lissus.

Tegleth- A Baazite general of Maruda, slain by Arrax at Erriad.

Zurlina- Great highland forest in the extreme upper regions of Elabaea.

About the Author

Phillip D. Campbell III (b. 1980) was born and raised in Southeast Michigan and currently resides in the city of Howell, midway between Lansing and Detroit. The *Tale of Manaeth* is the product of a lifelong love of fantasy, epic and history. Phillip received a BA in European History from Ave Maria University in 2005 and a certificate in Secondary Education at Madonna University in 2010. He is the Chairman of a high school writing club called the Penmoot Society, an amateur musician, an avid outdoorsman, as well as a husband and father of three.

Phillip is also a devout Roman Catholic and has a background in working with youth, teaching and writing about the Catholic faith and working for the restoration of Tradition within the Catholic Church. He can be reached for comments or questions at: phicampiii@taleofmanaeth.com.

Made in the USA
Lexington, KY
25 January 2017